The Heart's Map and the Mind's Compass

Aariv Wadhwa

Published by Aariv Wadhwa, 2024.

This is a work of fiction. Similarities to real people, places, or events are entirely coincidental.

THE HEART'S MAP AND THE MIND'S COMPASS

First edition. November 4, 2024.

Copyright © 2024 Aariv Wadhwa.

ISBN: 979-8227518224

Written by Aariv Wadhwa.

The Heart's Map and the Mind's Compass
Aariv Wadhwa

Preface

In a world that constantly demands decisions, we're often left wondering which voice to trust—the one in our heart or the one in our head. We're told to "follow our hearts" and chase our dreams, yet we're also urged to "be practical" and think things through. This duality has intrigued me for years. How can one navigate the vast landscape of life, balancing intuition with intellect, emotion with logic?

This story began as an exploration of that question. I wanted to create a world where this tug-of-war was given a physical form: a compass for logic and a heart map for feeling. Through Leo's journey, we see what happens when someone learns to balance these two forces, allowing each to inform the other, rather than letting one dominate. Leo's world may be a fantasy, yet the choices he faces are deeply real, echoing the daily decisions we make ourselves.

The Heart's Map and the Mind's Compass invites readers to consider that perhaps the most rewarding path forward isn't one that's clear-cut, but one that respects the wisdom in both the heart and the mind.

I hope you find meaning in Leo's story and that it helps you reflect on your own approach to life's many crossroads.

Chapter 1: The Cartographer's Compass

Chapter 2: The Heart's Call

Chapter 3: The Skeptical Scholar

Chapter 4: The Divergent Paths

Chapter 5: Wonders of the Heart

Chapter 6: The Dreamer's Perspective

Chapter 7: The Cliff of Choices

Chapter 8: Solon the Wanderer

Chapter 9: The Valley of Reflections

Chapter 10: The Hidden Glade

Chapter 11: The Crystal of Balance

Chapter 12: The Journey Back

Chapter 13: Mapping New Paths

Chapter 14: The New Pathfinders

Chapter 15: The Legacy of Balance

Epilogue: A New Compass, A New Map

Chapter 1: The Cartographer's Compass

In the quiet village of Eldergrove, nestled between ancient forests and rolling hills, everyone trusted their Compass. This wasn't an ordinary compass like one might use for hiking or sea navigation; the Compass of Eldergrove was a magical instrument, given to every person at birth. It was believed to carry the wisdom of reason, logic, and centuries of tradition. People lived their lives by it, trusting its steady, unwavering needle to guide them toward paths that were sensible, prudent, and safe.

Leo was no exception. From a young age, he had been fascinated by his Compass. Unlike many of his friends who only used it occasionally, Leo had developed an obsession for mastering its directions. As he grew older, he'd become the village cartographer, carefully drawing maps of Eldergrove and its surrounding lands, always guided by the logical paths his Compass suggested. His maps had earned him a reputation as someone deeply trustworthy and dependable; no one questioned his work. He was respected, even admired, for his commitment to precision.

Today, Leo sat at his workbench, meticulously adding new trails and paths to a map he was updating. His workshop was simple, filled with various inks, measuring tools, and sketches pinned to the walls. Each line on the map had to be exact, each curve calculated. His compass sat before him on the table, the needle pointing dutifully north. As he worked, his movements were calm, precise, and measured, mirroring the personality he'd developed over the years.

But even as he focused on his task, Leo's mind drifted to a curiosity he had long kept to himself: the Heart Map.

In Eldergrove, alongside the Compass, every person was also given a Heart Map—a small, folded piece of enchanted parchment that, if

THE HEART'S MAP AND THE MIND'S COMPASS 5

one were to believe the rumors, could glow with a faint light when one's feelings or desires suggested a path. But unlike the Compass, the Heart Map was a far more mysterious tool. Its paths were not visible to everyone, and even those who claimed to have seen it light up spoke of it with a kind of wonder tinged with fear. After all, a Heart Map could lead someone to unexpected, even dangerous, destinations, guided by little more than intuition and feeling.

Leo had never seen his own Heart Map glow, and he wasn't entirely sure he believed it ever would. "Emotions are too unpredictable," he often thought, "too likely to lead you astray." He kept his Heart Map folded and tucked away in a drawer. To Leo, it was an unnecessary tool, an old tradition that didn't fit with the reliability of his Compass.

As dusk settled over Eldergrove, Leo set down his quill, stretched, and looked out his workshop window. Outside, the village was winding down for the night. Lights began flickering in the homes, and families gathered around tables for evening meals. A peaceful silence fell over the village, broken only by the occasional murmur of laughter or conversation from the homes nearby.

But as Leo prepared to pack up for the night, a faint glow caught his eye. His gaze fell toward the drawer where his Heart Map lay, untouched and forgotten. And yet, there it was—a faint, barely noticeable light seeping through the drawer.

For a moment, he was frozen. "It can't be," he muttered. "I've never felt it glow before." He hesitated, his hand hovering over the drawer, his heart pounding. The rational part of him wanted to dismiss it, to ignore the glow and continue on as though nothing unusual had happened. But another part of him—a part he wasn't used to listening to—felt a surge of curiosity.

Slowly, almost reluctantly, Leo opened the drawer. The Heart Map lay there, glowing softly, its light pulsing like a heartbeat. With trembling fingers, he unfolded it, revealing a faint path that twisted and turned across the page. The path was unlike anything he'd ever seen before on his Compass or his maps. It was a route through the forest, leading far beyond the village, into a region known only in myths: the Lost Glade.

The Lost Glade was a place of legend in Eldergrove. Stories said it was a land hidden deep within the forest, accessible only by paths that appeared and vanished with the moonlight. Many in the village doubted its existence, dismissing it as a tale for children. But the few elders who spoke of it did so with a mixture of awe and fear, hinting that those who ventured into the Lost Glade might never return. No one had ever mapped it, and no Compass could lead you there.

Leo's pulse quickened. Why was his Heart Map guiding him to this place? What could it mean?

His logical mind immediately set to work analyzing the situation. "This could be a coincidence," he told himself, "or perhaps just an old charm in the Heart Map that has finally started to wear out." But even as he tried to dismiss it, a nagging curiosity persisted. Despite his attachment to reason, he couldn't shake the feeling that something significant was happening. For the first time in his life, the dependable paths of his Compass felt... limited.

He spent the night tossing and turning, unable to quiet his racing thoughts. Part of him wanted to set out at dawn, to follow the glowing path and see where it led. But another part warned him of the dangers, reminding him of his duty to the village, his responsibility as a cartographer. Following an unknown path seemed reckless, even foolish. And yet, his heart kept pulling him toward it.

The next morning, Leo returned to his workshop, bleary-eyed and weary but still drawn to the Heart Map. He spread it out on his desk, studying the route it showed. The faint light was still there, waiting, as if beckoning him to step outside the familiar lines he'd always followed.

A knock at the door interrupted his thoughts. It was Iris, the village elder and one of Leo's few confidants. She had taught him much of what he knew about cartography and the Compass, always emphasizing the importance of logic and careful planning. But Iris also had a keen sense of people's emotions, a trait that Leo admired but didn't fully understand.

"Good morning, Leo," Iris said as she entered, her sharp eyes taking in the Heart Map spread out on the desk. She raised an eyebrow. "You've finally unfolded it, I see."

Leo flushed, feeling as though he'd been caught in some secret act. "It... started glowing last night," he admitted, struggling to keep his tone casual. "I didn't expect it to show anything. I thought only the Compass showed real paths."

"Ah, the Compass may be reliable," Iris said with a soft smile, "but the Heart Map is the whisper of one's deeper self. Not all paths are visible to the eye alone, Leo. Sometimes, what we need lies beyond the paths we know."

Her words lingered in his mind long after she left. Could there really be paths worth exploring that logic couldn't explain? The question troubled him, shaking the foundation of everything he believed in.

For days, Leo wrestled with indecision. He went about his duties as usual, drawing maps, updating paths, and listening to villagers' requests. But the Heart Map's faint glow stayed with him, never dimming, always reminding him of the uncharted route waiting in the forest. It felt as though a doorway had opened in his mind, leading to a world he'd only glimpsed in stories.

Finally, he could resist no longer. One quiet evening, as the sun dipped below the horizon and the village settled into silence, Leo packed his supplies and took a deep breath. He had resolved to follow the Heart Map's path, if only for a short distance, just to see where it would lead. "I'll be back by dawn," he reassured himself, trying to quell the nervous excitement bubbling up within him.

Clutching his Compass in one hand and the Heart Map in the other, he set out into the forest. The familiar trails soon faded, and he found himself stepping onto a path that felt new, even foreign. The trees grew thicker, the air cooler, as though he were entering another realm altogether. His Compass, usually steady and clear, began to waver, its needle quivering uncertainly. But his Heart Map continued to glow, guiding him forward with a gentle, reassuring light.

As he ventured deeper into the woods, Leo felt a mix of exhilaration and fear. He was leaving behind the familiar, stepping into the unknown, trusting a path he couldn't fully understand. And yet, for the first time, he felt alive in a way he hadn't before. This wasn't just a map-making exercise; it was an adventure, a journey to discover something that defied reason.

In that moment, Leo realized that perhaps the Heart Map wasn't just showing him a physical route. It was guiding him to question, to see beyond the bounds of logic, to trust that there was value in paths that the Compass couldn't reveal. The Lost Glade awaited him, and with every step, Leo sensed that it held answers he couldn't yet comprehend.

As dawn approached, Leo reached a small clearing, a place unlike any he'd seen before. The trees sparkled with dew, the air was thick with the scent of wildflowers, and a gentle light bathed the scene in an otherworldly glow. He had found the edge of the Lost Glade. It was as beautiful as the legends had said, but there was something more—an energy, a sense of possibility that resonated within him.

Leo turned his gaze back toward the village, knowing that his journey was just beginning.

Chapter 2: The Heart's Call

In the quiet days that followed Leo's first encounter with the glow of his Heart Map, he found himself haunted by the memory of that mysterious light. Despite his logical, steadfast nature, he couldn't shake the sense that something profound was unfolding, an invitation from the unknown beckoning him toward paths he had only heard of in whispers. He wanted to dismiss it, to tuck away the Heart Map and focus on his tasks as he always had. Yet each day, he felt the faint pulse of the Heart Map calling to him, like a soft song just beyond his hearing, urging him to venture where his Compass would not lead.

Leo attempted to distract himself by doubling down on his work. He poured over the details of his maps, refining each line, every curve, ensuring that each path was as precise as possible. Eldergrove relied on these maps, and Leo took pride in his role as the village cartographer. But even as he worked, he caught himself glancing at the drawer where the Heart Map lay, its faint glow calling to him with an almost magnetic pull.

"*This is nonsense,*" he muttered to himself one evening, attempting to convince himself that the Heart Map was merely a distraction, an unnecessary complication. "*A whim, a superstition. I don't need it.*" And yet, he could feel the tension building within him, a growing restlessness that he couldn't ignore. His mind was trying to reason through it, to dismiss the Heart Map as fanciful nonsense, but his heart—ever steady—felt otherwise.

After several days of this internal tug-of-war, Leo found himself standing before Iris's home. He hadn't planned on coming here, but his feet had taken him to the village elder's door almost of their own accord. He hoped she might have some guidance, or perhaps even a way to help him forget about the Heart Map altogether. After all, if anyone understood both logic and mystery, it was Iris.

She greeted him warmly, sensing the unease written across his face. "You look like a man carrying a great weight," she said, inviting him in and pouring a warm tea that smelled faintly of lavender and mint.

Leo didn't waste any time with pleasantries. "Iris," he began, "I think there's something wrong with me." He quickly recounted the strange events of the past few days—the glow of the Heart Map, the relentless pull he felt, the battle between his desire to stay rooted in logic and his urge to explore.

Iris listened patiently, a serene smile on her face. "The Heart Map has found you, hasn't it?" she asked, her tone gentle, yet knowing.

Leo shifted uneasily. "I don't know what that means," he admitted. "I've never needed the Heart Map before. My Compass has always been enough." He hesitated. "But now... I can't ignore it. It's as if it's calling me to go somewhere—to see something that my Compass doesn't recognize."

Iris nodded, taking a slow sip of tea. "The Heart Map shows you paths that aren't always logical, Leo. Paths that call to a deeper part of yourself, beyond reason." Her eyes sparkled with an almost mischievous light. "Many of us spend our lives ignoring it, you know. But every once in a while, the Heart Map awakens, leading us to parts of ourselves we have yet to discover."

Her words resonated deeply with Leo, but his logical mind remained cautious. "And what if the Heart Map leads to danger?" he asked, his tone filled with genuine concern. "What if I lose my way?"

Iris placed a reassuring hand on his shoulder. "You may not know where the path will lead, but that's the nature of journeys that call to the heart. You'll have to trust that part of yourself, the part that longs for something beyond the familiar."

That night, Leo lay awake, pondering Iris's words. They stirred something in him, a sense that this journey might offer him more

THE HEART'S MAP AND THE MIND'S COMPASS   11

than just new paths on a map. But there was fear, too—the fear of leaving behind the comfort of logic and venturing into the unknown. He wrestled with this conflict for hours, his thoughts racing as he tried to reason through every potential outcome.

Eventually, exhaustion overtook him, and he drifted into a restless sleep. In his dreams, he found himself standing at the edge of a vast, misty forest, his Compass clutched tightly in one hand, the Heart Map glowing softly in the other. The path before him was shrouded, winding away into shadows and light, beckoning him forward. And as he stood there, the Heart Map's light grew stronger, illuminating the way even as his Compass quivered uncertainly.

When he awoke, the decision had already been made. He would follow the call, step beyond the boundaries of comfort and reason, if only to see where the Heart Map led.

The following morning, Leo rose early, his resolve bolstered by the clarity that comes only with dawn. He packed a small satchel with his map tools, a notebook, and a few essentials—a canteen, some bread, a small knife for protection. He didn't know how long he would be gone, but he prepared as best as he could, bringing along items that might be useful if he ventured deep into the forest.

As he packed, his hands trembled slightly. Despite his resolution, he still felt a knot of anxiety tightening in his chest. This journey was unlike anything he had ever attempted. Each map he had drawn, every trail he had charted, had been grounded in the familiar. Now, he was stepping into uncharted territory, guided not by the clarity of his Compass but by the soft, enigmatic glow of the Heart Map.

Before leaving, he took a final look around his workshop. It was filled with the tools and maps that represented his life's work—a life he cherished, built on logic, precision, and order. But now, standing on the edge of something unknown, he felt a pang of doubt. *"Am I really ready for this?"* he asked himself.

But the glow of the Heart Map persisted, casting a warm light that seemed to whisper words of encouragement. Taking a deep breath, Leo closed the workshop door behind him and set off.

The forest surrounding Eldergrove was familiar territory. Leo had mapped these paths countless times, knew each bend and turn, each tree and clearing. But as he ventured further from the village, guided by the light of the Heart Map rather than his Compass, he found himself moving beyond the familiar trails and into areas that were rarely traveled.

The forest grew denser, the trees towering above him like ancient sentinels guarding secrets known only to the woods. The air was thick with the scent of pine and earth, and sunlight filtered through the leaves, casting dappled shadows on the forest floor. As he walked, the Heart Map's light pulsed in rhythm with his footsteps, guiding him down narrow paths that twisted and turned unexpectedly, as though the very forest were rearranging itself to lead him forward.

He passed through clearings he had never seen, crossed streams that sparkled under the sunlight, and even stumbled upon small groves of wildflowers in vibrant shades of blue, yellow, and purple. Each step carried him deeper into a world he had not known existed, a world that seemed alive with possibilities and mysteries.

As the hours passed, Leo found himself feeling an odd mixture of calm and exhilaration. The logic-driven part of him worried about losing his way, but his heart felt alive, attuned to the pulse of the Heart Map. It was as though he were rediscovering a forgotten part of himself, a part that yearned for exploration, for freedom beyond the boundaries of rationality.

By late afternoon, Leo came to a small clearing where the trees formed a natural archway overhead, creating a canopy that dappled the ground with light and shadow. Here, he paused to rest, sipping from his canteen and catching his breath. As he did, he became aware of a faint rustling in the bushes nearby.

At first, he dismissed it as the wind. But then he saw movement—a pair of curious eyes peering out at him from behind a tree. Startled, he reached for his small knife, but before he could react further, a figure stepped into view: a young woman, dressed in simple, earth-toned clothes, her hair wild and her eyes sharp with intelligence and curiosity.

"Who are you?" she asked, her gaze flicking to the Heart Map glowing faintly in his hand. "What brings you to these parts?"

Leo stammered for a moment, surprised by the sudden encounter. "I... I'm Leo. I'm from Eldergrove," he managed, still clutching his Heart Map. "I'm... following a path."

The woman's eyes softened, and she smiled, as though understanding something he had yet to grasp. "You're following your Heart Map," she said simply. "It's rare to see someone who actually listens to it. Most people ignore it, relying on their Compasses alone."

Her words resonated with him, though he felt a twinge of defensiveness. "My Compass has served me well," he replied. "It's kept me safe, helped me find my way."

The woman nodded. "Compasses are useful, yes. But they only show paths that are already known, paths that others have walked before. The Heart Map... it leads you to places only you can discover."

Her words stirred something deep within Leo, a sense that he was on the brink of an understanding that would change him. But before he could respond, the woman motioned for him to follow her. "Come," she said. "There's something you need to see."

The woman led Leo through a series of winding paths that seemed to appear only as they walked. Finally, they arrived at a small, hidden glade surrounded by towering trees and filled with an ethereal light. At the center of the glade stood a series of stone mirrors, their surfaces polished to a perfect sheen, reflecting the sunlight in a way that made them appear almost alive.

"This is the Glade of Mirrors," the woman explained. "Each mirror shows you a different path—some guided by logic, others by the heart."

Leo approached the mirrors cautiously, gazing into each one. In one, he saw a reflection of himself, following his Compass, his life steady, predictable, safe. In another, he saw a version of himself guided solely by his Heart Map, venturing into unknown territories, facing challenges and wonders he had never imagined.

For a long time, Leo stood there, caught between the two reflections. The safe path and the wild one. The mind and the heart. He realized that his journey was not merely about following one or the other, but about understanding when to let each guide him.

The woman's voice broke the silence. "The journey ahead will test you, Leo. It will ask you to choose, again and again, between the Compass and the Heart Map. But only by embracing both will you find the path that is truly yours."

As Leo left the Glade of Mirrors that evening, his mind was filled with questions, but his heart felt a newfound resolve. The Heart's Call was growing stronger, and he knew that his journey had only just begun.

Chapter 3: The Skeptical Scholar

As Leo continued his journey into the heart of the forest, guided by the soft glow of his Heart Map, he found his thoughts constantly shifting between the familiarity of his Compass and the unpredictable pull of the path he now walked. The landscape around him grew stranger, more enchanting with each step—lush groves, bubbling brooks, and patches of wildflowers he had never seen before. The Heart Map seemed to know secrets he could only discover by following it.

It was during one such walk, as Leo marveled at the wonders surrounding him, that he encountered someone who would alter the course of his journey: Iris, a scholar from Eldergrove whom he had only known from a distance. Iris was known for her sharp intellect and unshakable commitment to logic and reason. If there was anyone who embodied the principles of the Compass, it was her.

Leo spotted Iris seated on a fallen tree trunk, a book balanced on her knee, her expression thoughtful yet stern. Her presence here surprised him, and for a moment he wondered if she had followed him. Then he realized it was pure coincidence—or perhaps fate, though he knew Iris would scoff at the idea.

She looked up as he approached, her gaze scrutinizing. "Leo? What on earth are you doing here, wandering about like this?"

Leo hesitated, unsure how to explain his journey. "I... felt drawn here," he said at last, carefully avoiding mentioning the Heart Map. "I wanted to explore beyond the usual paths."

Iris raised an eyebrow, unimpressed. "Drawn? Are you saying you left your Compass behind?" She folded her arms, frowning. "I thought you were one of the more sensible ones."

"I didn't leave my Compass," Leo replied, pulling it out to show her. "But I'm trying something new. Sometimes, the Compass doesn't show everything." He hesitated, feeling a strange sense of vulnerability. "There are things in the world that can't be found with logic alone."

Iris's frown deepened. "Logic is precisely what keeps us safe, Leo. It's what separates us from chaos. We rely on our Compasses because they guide us on known paths, paths that don't lead to danger or confusion."

They fell into step together, with Leo feeling a mixture of intrigue and caution. He respected Iris's intelligence and knew her to be a voice of reason, yet he felt a tug in his heart urging him to continue on this path, to see where the Heart Map would take him.

As they walked, Leo found himself growing increasingly aware of the quiet yet persistent glow of his Heart Map. It pulled him toward an offshoot of the path they were on, a narrow trail barely visible through the dense undergrowth. He felt a spark of curiosity but glanced at Iris, wondering if she would join him.

"Let's go this way," he suggested, pointing to the narrow trail.

Iris glanced at the path, a skeptical look on her face. "That's not on any map, Leo. It could lead to dead ends, or worse."

Leo tried to explain, though he knew his words might sound foolish. "Sometimes, the best discoveries come from taking a step off the known path."

Iris sighed. "That's exactly the problem with these Heart Maps everyone keeps talking about. They lead people into nonsense, into places with no purpose or logic. A Compass doesn't lead you to distractions; it keeps you focused, grounded."

But Leo, feeling an irresistible pull, took a step onto the narrow path, and to his relief, Iris followed, albeit reluctantly. As they walked, the forest opened up around them, revealing a small glade filled with a field of delicate white flowers. Their petals glistened as though dusted with starlight, shimmering in the gentle sunlight filtering through the canopy.

Leo stopped, taking in the sight. He felt a sense of wonder, a silent awe at the unexpected beauty of this hidden place. But beside him, Iris remained unmoved, her expression unchanged.

"Beautiful, perhaps," she admitted grudgingly, "but pointless. A place like this has no value to anyone except a poet." She shook her head. "We should stick to the paths we know are reliable, not get distracted by every pretty scene."

Leo looked at her, surprised at her disinterest. "Not everything has to have a practical purpose, Iris. Some things are valuable just because they exist, because they remind us of something larger than ourselves."

She scoffed slightly, brushing her hand dismissively at the field of flowers. "Spoken like someone who's losing touch with reason. What you call beauty, I call a waste of time. This forest is full of plants and flowers—there's nothing special about these."

But as she spoke, Leo noticed something about the flowers. Each one seemed to be slightly different, with a unique pattern on its petals, a detail he might have missed had he not stopped to look closer. "Have you ever noticed," he began, "that each flower has its own pattern? They're not identical, even though they're all part of the same field. Isn't that remarkable?"

Iris shrugged, unwilling to be drawn in. "Just another product of nature's random variations. The Compass leads us to certainty, Leo. It takes us away from trivialities like this."

They walked on, and for a time they were silent. Leo could feel a subtle tension between them, a friction created by their opposing perspectives. He felt compelled to continue on this path, to let his Heart Map lead, but Iris's words reminded him of the comfort and clarity of logic. Logic was safe, predictable; it was what he had always known.

The narrow trail eventually led them to a gentle, bubbling stream. Sunlight danced on the surface of the water, casting ripples of light across the forest floor. Leo paused by the stream, dipping his hand into the cool, clear water, savoring the feeling of refreshment.

"Look," he said to Iris, gesturing to the stream. "Even water flows freely, without rigid boundaries. It finds its own path."

She rolled her eyes. "Water flows because it follows the path of least resistance. It doesn't choose its course; it follows the laws of gravity and physics." She shook her head, exasperated. "That's what you're missing, Leo—nature has laws, logic. It isn't driven by whims and feelings."

"Maybe," he replied, "but isn't there room for a bit of wonder too? For stepping outside the lines we draw for ourselves?"

Iris crossed her arms, her tone firm. "Wonder doesn't get us anywhere, Leo. It leads to foolishness, to decisions made on emotion rather than reason. This Heart Map of yours—it's leading you away from what's real and into illusions."

Leo felt a flash of frustration. He respected Iris and her dedication to knowledge, but her dismissiveness stung. "Maybe that's true for you," he said, "but I'm finding that sometimes logic alone isn't enough. The Heart Map is helping me see things I would've missed otherwise."

She sighed, giving him a weary look. "Leo, you're a cartographer, a person who creates maps to help others find their way. You have a responsibility to stay grounded in reality. People depend on you."

Her words struck a chord, and for a moment he questioned himself. Was he being reckless? Was he endangering himself—and possibly others—by straying from the logical, clear paths the Compass provided?

But then, in his heart, he felt a stirring that he couldn't ignore. He thought of Iris's focus on predictability, the way she dismissed

THE HEART'S MAP AND THE MIND'S COMPASS 19

anything that couldn't be explained by logic. It made sense, but it felt incomplete, as if it left something vital behind.

The conversation continued as they walked, both of them presenting their arguments, neither willing to yield. They traveled deeper into the forest, and Leo noticed that the landscape had shifted subtly. The trees grew taller, the canopy thicker, and the sounds of the forest more vibrant. He could sense the magic in the air, as though the forest itself recognized the conflict between them.

At last, they arrived at a secluded clearing where an ancient tree stood, its trunk twisted and gnarled, branches spreading out like the arms of a wise elder. Leo felt drawn to it, sensing an energy he couldn't quite explain. "This tree," he whispered, almost to himself. "There's something... profound about it."

Iris studied the tree with a skeptical eye. "It's an old tree, yes. But it's just a tree, Leo. A part of the natural world, like everything else here."

"But it's more than that," Leo insisted. He stepped closer, placing his hand on the tree's rough bark. A warmth seeped into his palm, as though the tree were alive in a way he couldn't fully understand. "This tree has been here for centuries, maybe longer. It's seen more than we could imagine."

Iris folded her arms, unimpressed. "Stories and sentiment, Leo. That's all this Heart Map nonsense is leading you to. Stories and sentiment are the foundations of illusion, not reality."

Her words echoed through his mind, challenging the feeling that had blossomed in his chest. But as he stood there, touching the ancient tree, he felt a sudden surge of clarity. He realized that both perspectives—logic and emotion, the Compass and the Heart Map—had value. They were not opposites but complementary forces, each guiding him in a different way.

After a long silence, Leo turned to Iris, his voice calm but resolute. "Iris, I understand your perspective. Logic is what has kept us safe, given us structure and order. But I believe there's more to life than just structure. Sometimes, we have to let our hearts guide us, to explore paths that logic alone can't show us."

Iris's expression softened slightly, though her skepticism remained. "You may be right, Leo. But be careful. Paths of the heart are often shrouded in mist. They're beautiful, yes, but they can also lead to places we never intended to go."

They exchanged a quiet farewell, both of them feeling the weight of the choices that lay ahead. As Iris turned and disappeared down the well-worn path, Leo looked at his Heart Map, its glow growing brighter. With a deep breath, he set out once again, following the call of the unknown, embracing the journey that lay before him.

Chapter 4: The Divergent Paths

As Leo and Iris continued their journey through the dense forest, they walked in a quiet yet tense silence. The clash between his reliance on his Heart Map and her dedication to the Compass remained fresh in both of their minds, like an unspoken argument that neither had truly won. The path ahead was narrow and twisting, the air thick with the earthy scent of moss and ancient trees.

They had been walking for hours, the forest growing increasingly unfamiliar with each step, when they finally reached a fork in the road. It was a subtle split at first, where the path curved off in two opposite directions, each disappearing into the shadowed green depths of the forest. One path was clearly marked by carefully arranged stones and sturdy trees standing like silent guards along the way; the other was wilder, with untamed foliage spilling over the path and a hint of something more mysterious.

Instinctively, Leo pulled out his Heart Map, feeling the faint glow it emitted pulse stronger. It was as if the map itself was alive, attuned to the quiet rhythm of his heart, guiding him toward the unknown. The light on his Heart Map clearly illuminated the wilder, less-defined path. He felt an inexplicable tug towards it, a silent call whispering to him.

Beside him, Iris unclipped her Compass, which pointed firmly in the opposite direction. She held it up, raising an eyebrow at him. "This way," she said simply, her voice steady and certain as ever. "The Compass is clear."

Leo hesitated, glancing down at his Heart Map. The glow had never been this strong, and he felt his curiosity grow. His fingers traced the faint lines that appeared to pulse with a life of their own, leading him along the unmarked, shadowed path. He glanced at Iris, whose expression was a mix of challenge and mild exasperation.

"Leo, let's not make this difficult. The Compass knows the safe route," she said, her tone leaving little room for argument. "Your... Heart Map may seem compelling, but it's just playing with your emotions. Trust me, the Compass doesn't make mistakes."

He looked back at the wild path, feeling torn. He knew the Compass would lead them along a well-trodden, predictable path. Safe, reliable, and familiar. But something inside him refused to turn away from the glow of his Heart Map. "I can't ignore this, Iris. The Heart Map is guiding me here for a reason, I feel it."

Iris sighed, her expression growing more frustrated. "The Compass has guided our people for generations, Leo. It doesn't lead us into danger or down pointless paths. You're letting your emotions cloud your judgment."

"Maybe," he admitted, feeling the weight of her words. But he also knew that if he ignored his Heart Map now, he might never fully understand what it was trying to show him. "But this is something I need to see for myself."

She shook her head, clearly doubtful. "Fine," she said, exhaling sharply. "I'll go with you. But don't expect me to follow blindly. I'll be here to point out every mistake you make."

He gave her a small, appreciative smile. "That's all I could ask for."

With that, they took their first step onto the unmarked path, setting off into the unknown.

The path they chose was rugged, barely discernible beneath the dense forest floor. Branches stretched across the trail like wild arms, and vines twisted their way through thick shrubs, blocking parts of the way forward. Despite the difficulty, Leo felt an unusual sense of anticipation, an excitement that he couldn't quite put into words. The Heart Map continued to glow faintly in his hand, and he found himself trusting its light more and more with each step.

Iris, on the other hand, was less enthusiastic. She cast skeptical glances at the map and questioned nearly every turn. "Are you sure this isn't leading us in circles?" she asked, her voice tinged with frustration. "We've been walking for hours, and I don't see any signs that we're getting anywhere."

"It may not be the most direct path," Leo conceded, "but sometimes journeys aren't just about reaching a destination. They're about what we learn along the way."

Iris raised an eyebrow. "Philosophical, are we? That's all well and good in theory, but it's not going to help if we're lost in the middle of nowhere."

Leo sighed, understanding her frustration but unwilling to give up on the path his Heart Map was showing. "I know you don't see the purpose in this, but I can't turn back. I've spent my whole life following the Compass, taking the paths everyone else took. This feels different."

They continued in silence, and as they did, Leo noticed subtle details along the way—the faint whisper of wind through the trees, the vibrant colors of moss that covered the stones, and the way small animals peeked out from their hiding places as they passed. He felt alive, connected to the forest in a way he hadn't experienced before. The Heart Map seemed to glow brighter, almost as if it were acknowledging his growing confidence in its guidance.

But Iris was still uneasy, and every so often, she would pause, glancing back in the direction of the main path. "This is foolishness," she muttered at one point, just loud enough for him to hear. "Emotions cloud judgment, Leo. You're letting some strange impulse lead you away from what's known, from what's safe."

"Maybe," he said, choosing his words carefully. "But sometimes, maybe it's worth taking a step off the safe path."

As they ventured deeper, the path began to narrow, and the forest grew darker, with towering trees casting long shadows over them. The foliage was dense, and they had to push through tangles of branches and vines that seemed to reach out to hinder their progress. The sounds of the forest grew louder, more intense, and an air of mystery surrounded them, as though they were being watched by unseen eyes.

Eventually, they reached a small clearing where a shallow creek flowed, its water glistening in the dappled sunlight. Leo knelt down, dipping his hand into the cool water, feeling refreshed. The Heart Map pulsed in his hand, its glow faintly illuminating the surroundings, casting a gentle light across the water.

Iris crossed her arms, watching him with a look of barely concealed skepticism. "This is where your Heart Map has brought us? A creek in the middle of nowhere?"

"It's more than just a creek," he replied, gesturing to the way the water sparkled as if touched by stardust. "Look closer. There's something here—something hidden in plain sight."

She sighed, rolling her eyes, but knelt beside him nonetheless. Together, they observed the way the light danced across the water, forming intricate patterns. As they watched, they noticed faint symbols appearing in the ripples—ancient symbols that Leo recognized from his studies but had never seen in the wild.

Iris's eyes widened in surprise. "These symbols... they're from the old maps. How are they here?"

He looked at her, sensing a slight shift in her demeanor. "I don't know. But this is exactly why I needed to follow this path. The Compass didn't lead us here, but the Heart Map did. Sometimes, following our hearts shows us things that logic alone can't reveal."

Iris was silent, her gaze fixed on the symbols. It was as though a part of her was beginning to understand, to see value in what she had dismissed.

They continued onward, moving away from the creek and deeper into the forest. As they walked, the Heart Map's glow grew even stronger, guiding them forward. The air around them seemed charged with anticipation, as if they were on the brink of something significant.

THE HEART'S MAP AND THE MIND'S COMPASS

Finally, they reached another fork in the path. Leo's Heart Map glowed brightly toward the left path, while Iris's Compass pointed firmly to the right. They both stopped, staring down their respective paths in silence.

"This is where our paths truly diverge," Leo murmured, feeling a pang of uncertainty.

Iris looked at him, her expression unreadable. "You know where I stand, Leo. The Compass has guided us for generations, and it hasn't failed yet. But if you're determined to follow that... Heart Map of yours, this is where we part ways."

Leo felt a moment of doubt. She was right; the Compass had always provided a reliable way forward. But something inside him, some inner voice he couldn't ignore, urged him to continue along the path his Heart Map showed.

"I have to follow this, Iris," he said quietly. "I don't expect you to understand, but I know this is where I'm meant to go."

To his surprise, she hesitated. There was a flicker of something in her eyes, something that looked almost like curiosity. She sighed deeply, as though exasperated with herself. "Fine," she said, her voice laced with reluctance. "I'll go with you. But only to see where this path leads—and to keep you from getting yourself into trouble."

Relief flooded through him, and he nodded, grateful. Together, they turned and took their first steps onto the left path, the path illuminated by the glow of the Heart Map.

As they continued along the path, they encountered sights and sounds unlike anything they had seen before. They passed through a grove where fireflies danced in broad daylight, their soft glow creating a gentle, dreamlike atmosphere. Strange, beautiful plants grew along the path, their colors vibrant and their petals soft to the touch.

Iris seemed awed despite herself, her skepticism temporarily forgotten. "I've never seen anything like this," she murmured, touching one of the plants. "This... this wasn't on any map I've ever seen."

Leo smiled, feeling a quiet sense of satisfaction. "That's the beauty of following the heart. It shows us things we would never find if we only followed the familiar."

For the first time, Iris didn't have a reply. She simply walked beside him, taking in the wonders around them, her eyes filled with an unspoken wonder.

The two walked deeper into the forest, the glow of the Heart Map guiding them forward.

Chapter 5: Wonders of the Heart

The sun was high in the sky as Leo and Iris walked further along the unmarked trail. The thick forest canopy filtered the sunlight, casting dappled patches of light and shadow across the path. Despite Iris's usual skepticism, the Heart Map's path had already shown them marvels beyond what either could have anticipated. Their steps fell into an unspoken rhythm, their shared silence a truce of sorts—she, the logical scholar, and he, the heart-led cartographer, moving forward together into the unknown.

They soon found themselves standing at the edge of an expansive clearing. Leo felt the Heart Map's pulse grow stronger, as if urging him forward, and a shiver of anticipation ran through him. He glanced over at Iris, who raised a skeptical eyebrow but seemed willing to indulge his next steps. They stepped through the final barrier of trees and entered the clearing.

Before them lay a lake so clear and tranquil it seemed otherworldly. Leo's breath caught in his chest. The surface of the lake mirrored the sky perfectly, a still, liquid pane of glass. Yet, despite it being midday, the reflection wasn't simply of the bright blue sky above. Instead, stars twinkled in the depths, constellations woven together in patterns he had only seen at night. He felt as though he was looking into another world—a place where the boundary between day and night had blurred into something timeless.

"Is this real?" Iris whispered, her eyes wide with awe. She looked around, her usual air of certainty replaced with an uncharacteristic wonder.

Leo took a step forward, entranced. "I... I think so. This is beyond anything I've ever imagined."

He knelt at the edge of the lake, extending a tentative hand toward the water's surface. As his fingers brushed against it, ripples spread out, disturbing the starlit reflection, yet no light scattered; instead, the stars seemed to dance within the ripples, shimmering with renewed intensity. Leo's mind raced with questions, but in his heart, he felt a deep, inexplicable peace. This was exactly where he was supposed to be.

Iris joined him at the water's edge, her usual guarded expression replaced with a look of genuine wonder. "It defies logic," she said, almost to herself. "Stars in the daylight? A lake reflecting constellations? There's no way to explain this."

"Maybe that's the point," Leo replied softly. "Maybe not everything needs an explanation."

She turned to him, skepticism still lingering but less pronounced. "That's easy to say, but I can't just abandon logic. It's... it's part of how I understand the world. And yet..." Her voice trailed off as her gaze returned to the shimmering lake. "This place is beautiful. I'll admit that much."

Leo smiled, feeling a surge of satisfaction. It wasn't exactly a victory, but the fact that Iris had acknowledged the beauty of something inexplicable was a step. He felt a warmth blossom in his chest, a shared moment that transcended their differences. For a moment, it was enough just to be here, marveling at the wonders his Heart Map had led them to.

As they stood there, lost in the lake's mesmerizing beauty, Leo felt a slight stirring in the air behind him. The forest, which had been so still and silent, suddenly came alive with the soft rustle of leaves and the faint padding of something moving closer. Iris stiffened, her hand instinctively reaching toward her Compass.

From the shadows, a figure emerged, a creature unlike any they had ever seen. It was small, with fur the color of moonlight and eyes that shimmered like tiny galaxies. Its movements were fluid, as though it glided over the forest floor without disturbing a single leaf. The creature's gaze was calm and wise, and as it approached, it exuded an aura of gentle curiosity.

Leo and Iris exchanged a glance, unsure of how to respond. The creature looked at them intently, then tilted its head, as if studying their expressions. Leo felt a strange sense of kinship with it, as if it somehow understood him on a level that words could never reach.

"What is it?" Iris asked, her voice a mix of fascination and caution.

"I don't know," Leo replied, keeping his voice soft. He felt an odd pull toward the creature, like an invitation to connect. Slowly, he extended a hand, palm up, hoping to convey his friendly intentions. The creature observed him for a moment, then took a step closer, touching its nose to his hand.

At that touch, Leo felt a rush of emotions and sensations flooding into him—an understanding of the forest, of the world beyond maps and charts. It was as though the creature shared a part of its essence with him, a gift of intuition that bypassed logic and reached straight into his heart.

"Can you understand us?" Leo whispered, almost afraid to break the delicate connection.

The creature blinked slowly, then stepped back, nodding with a grace that felt almost human. It turned its gaze to Iris, studying her with the same calm intensity. She shifted uncomfortably, but something in the creature's eyes seemed to soften her stance. After a moment, she exhaled, lowering her guard.

"What... what do you want from us?" she asked, her voice barely above a whisper.

The creature tilted its head, its expression serene. Then, in a gesture as clear as any words, it pointed with its paw toward the Heart Map in Leo's hand, as if acknowledging the journey they were on. It seemed to be telling them that the path they were following was one of great importance, a path that held wonders they had only begun to uncover.

As they continued to stare at the creature, it began to move along the lakeside, glancing back at them as if urging them to follow. Leo felt the familiar tug of the Heart Map, and without hesitation, he took a step forward, trusting that this creature would lead them to something remarkable. Iris, after a brief pause, followed him, her expression a mixture of curiosity and caution.

The creature led them along the edge of the lake, weaving between trees and moss-covered stones, until they reached a secluded spot where the forest opened up into another small clearing. In the center of the clearing stood a cluster of strange, luminous flowers that emitted a gentle, soothing light. They seemed to pulse with the same rhythm as the stars in the lake, their soft glow casting a warm radiance over the clearing.

Leo's eyes widened as he took in the sight. "I never knew such beauty existed here," he murmured, captivated by the ethereal flowers.

"These flowers... they're incredible," Iris said, her voice filled with genuine awe. "I've studied hundreds of plant species, but I've never seen anything like this."

The creature padded forward, nudging one of the flowers with its nose. To Leo's surprise, the flower responded, opening up like a delicate lantern, revealing tiny star-like seeds inside that twinkled with a soft, mesmerizing glow. It was as if each seed held a fragment of the night sky.

Leo felt his Heart Map pulse in response, and a sense of purpose filled him. This was why he had followed the path. The lake, the creature, the flowers—each one a piece of a larger, more profound tapestry that went beyond anything he could map. It was a reminder that the world held wonders that couldn't be captured on paper, that sometimes, the journey itself was the destination.

They sat beside the luminous flowers, the creature settling comfortably beside them. Leo felt a quiet peace, as if he had found something he had been searching for his entire life, even if he hadn't known it. He looked over at Iris, who had taken out her notebook, scribbling notes as quickly as her hand would allow.

"Iris," he said softly, breaking the silence. "Do you see now why I had to follow the Heart Map? Why I couldn't ignore it?"

She looked up from her notes, meeting his gaze. For a moment, she was silent, her usual sharpness softened by a newfound understanding. "I think I do," she admitted, her voice barely audible. "This place... it defies everything I thought I knew. And yet, it's beautiful in a way that logic alone could never capture."

Leo nodded, feeling a surge of gratitude that she was beginning to understand. "I'm not saying the Compass is wrong. It has its purpose, its place. But sometimes, there are things we can only find by following the heart."

She studied him, a hint of a smile tugging at her lips. "You're still a bit foolish, you know. But maybe... maybe there's wisdom in your foolishness."

They shared a quiet laugh, a moment of connection that bridged the gap between their different perspectives. In that moment, Leo felt a profound gratitude—not just for the wonders he had discovered, but for the companionship he had found along the way. He glanced at the creature, which watched them with a serene expression, as if satisfied with their newfound understanding.

As they prepared to leave the clearing, the creature approached them, its gaze warm and wise. It raised a paw, pressing it against Leo's chest, right above his heart. He felt a warmth spread through him, a gentle reminder to always listen to the quiet voice within, to follow the path of wonder wherever it might lead.

Leo looked down at the Heart Map in his hand, the glow softer now but steady, as though it had guided him to exactly where he needed to be. He felt a sense of gratitude toward the creature and bowed his head, acknowledging the silent lesson it had imparted.

Iris, too, gave a nod of respect to the creature, her eyes shining with a mixture of awe and gratitude. "Thank you," she said softly, her voice laced with genuine appreciation.

Together, they walked back toward the main path, leaving the lake and its starry reflection behind. The creature watched them until they disappeared into the trees, its presence a lingering reminder of the beauty that awaited those who dared to follow the call of the heart.

As they emerged from the clearing, Leo glanced back one last time, a quiet promise forming in his mind. No matter where his journey led him, he would remember this place, this moment, and the lesson it had taught him: that there was a world beyond the maps, a world of wonder and beauty that only the heart could reveal.

With a final glance at Iris, who seemed deep in thought, Leo smiled. The path before them was still unknown, still full of questions, but he felt ready to face it. For the first time in his life, he felt truly alive, his heart open to the wonders of the world.

Chapter 6: The Dreamer's Perspective

Leo and Iris were still marveling over the hidden lake with its star-like reflections, the encounter with the creature, and the wisdom the journey had revealed. Each step along the path guided by Leo's Heart Map felt like a leap into the unknown. But this leap, while filled with uncertainty, was also rich with wonder. Iris seemed more open now, no longer casting immediate judgment on the things they encountered, though her cautious nature still held her back from fully embracing the heart-led journey.

As they continued their trek, they reached a dense forest filled with tall, whispering trees whose branches intertwined overhead, forming a natural cathedral. Sunlight streamed through in golden beams, creating pockets of warmth amid the cool shadows. Leo felt an unusual pull in his Heart Map—a gentle, almost musical pulse. Curious, he held it out in front of him, trying to sense where it wanted him to go.

The forest ahead opened up to reveal a small, sunlit clearing. There, a man sat on a fallen tree, surrounded by a sea of wildflowers. He held a battered guitar, strumming it softly while singing to himself, lost in his own world. His clothes were mismatched and worn, his hair a wild mane of curls, and his face was lit up with a carefree smile. He didn't have a Compass, nor did he seem to be following any map. He was simply... there, basking in the day's warmth.

Noticing their presence, the man looked up, his smile widening. "Ah, travelers! Welcome to my little oasis," he said, setting his guitar aside and giving them a wave.

Leo stepped forward, drawn by the man's warmth and openness. "Hello. I'm Leo, and this is Iris." He motioned toward his companion, who had paused just outside the clearing, looking at the stranger with a cautious expression.

"Leo and Iris!" the man exclaimed, as if delighted to hear their names. "Wonderful names for wonderful people. I'm Callum." He extended a hand, which Leo shook eagerly.

Iris hesitated, her eyes scanning Callum with a mixture of curiosity and concern. "Nice to meet you," she said carefully, crossing her arms. "You don't have a Compass?"

Callum laughed, shaking his head. "No, no Compass for me. Never needed one, really. I travel where the wind takes me, where the flowers bloom brightest, and where the songs are sweetest." He gestured to the wildflowers surrounding him. "This place, for instance—I've stayed here for days, just soaking in the beauty."

Leo's eyes widened in admiration, and he glanced back at Iris, who looked both skeptical and somewhat unnerved.

Leo felt a kindred spirit in Callum, sensing that the musician was a rare soul who lived in pure alignment with his heart. There was a spontaneity about him, a joy and freedom that seemed almost magical. "So... you don't use any guides?" Leo asked, trying to understand the concept.

Callum chuckled, picking up his guitar again. "Guides? No, no. I've got my heart, and that's all I need. My heart tells me where to go, what to do, and when to stop. Sometimes, I get lost, but that's part of the fun. You discover things you'd never find on a map."

Iris cleared her throat. "But how do you know you're going anywhere at all? I mean, without direction, without structure... aren't you just... wandering?"

Callum shrugged, unbothered by her question. "Wandering, maybe. But life's meant to be wandered through, isn't it? I find what I need along the way. Sometimes, it's a meal shared with a stranger. Other times, it's a song waiting to be written." He strummed his guitar again, his fingers dancing over the strings as though they moved on their own.

Leo felt a thrill at Callum's words, an invitation to let go of control and embrace the unknown. There was an allure to the idea of traveling solely by intuition, of living without the rigid structures that the Compass or even the Heart Map imposed. He looked at Iris, wondering what she thought of this man whose philosophy was so vastly different from her own.

Iris's brow furrowed, her lips pursed in thought. "That may work for you, Callum, but not everyone can live like that. Some of us need structure to feel secure, to have purpose."

Callum smiled, a twinkle in his eye. "Purpose? What could be more purposeful than being fully alive in each moment? That's all the purpose I need." He gestured to the clearing around them, his voice softening. "If I hadn't followed my heart here, I wouldn't have found this grove, wouldn't have met you both. Sometimes, letting go of direction is the best way to find what you truly need."

Iris seemed unconvinced but also captivated. She watched Callum closely, her gaze softening as he strummed a gentle tune that floated through the clearing like a breeze.

Callum eventually set down his guitar and stood, stretching his arms overhead. "Shall we explore the grove? I've found some of the most amazing flowers just a little further in. It's a magical place, if you're willing to let go of the path."

Leo eagerly nodded, feeling a growing excitement. He looked at Iris, hoping she'd join them, but she hesitated, her wariness showing. Finally, with a sigh, she followed, her steps slower, her gaze focused on every detail around them as though searching for the logic in the lush, untamed beauty of the grove.

Callum led them deeper into the grove, his movements loose and carefree. He picked wildflowers as they walked, handing them to Leo and Iris with a grin. "Each flower has a story, you know," he said, twirling one of the delicate blooms between his fingers. "This one? It was probably kissed by the morning dew, blessed by the first light of dawn. And this one…" He handed Leo a particularly vibrant red flower.

"This one's got a wild spirit. It grew in a place where no flower should have grown. But it did anyway, strong and free."

Leo accepted the flower, feeling a rush of admiration for Callum's perspective. It was as if each thing Callum encountered held a mystery, a piece of magic waiting to be uncovered. Iris, however, remained distant, observing him with a guarded expression.

"So you believe the flowers have... spirits?" Iris asked, a hint of skepticism in her voice.

"Why not?" Callum replied easily. "Everything's alive, in its own way. If you listen closely, you can feel it. The world speaks, Iris. You just have to be willing to hear it." He paused, glancing back at her with a gentle smile. "Even if it doesn't always make sense."

Iris shook her head, but a small smile tugged at the corner of her mouth. "I suppose I can appreciate the poetry of it, at least."

They continued their journey, the grove growing denser, filled with an even greater variety of wildflowers, their colors vibrant and almost otherworldly. Leo felt as if they had stepped into a hidden realm, a world untouched by the usual rules. He felt his Heart Map pulse faintly, guiding him, but he was so caught up in the beauty around him that he barely noticed.

Callum's laughter echoed through the trees as he dashed ahead, twirling and leaping, entirely immersed in his own joy. Leo followed him with a grin, feeling lighter than he ever had. But after a while, he realized he could no longer see the path they had come from. He stopped, looking around. The grove, which had once seemed inviting and beautiful, now felt vast and disorienting.

"Iris?" Leo called, noticing her a few steps behind, her gaze darting around as she too realized how far they had wandered.

"Callum!" she shouted, her voice edged with irritation and worry. "Where are you leading us?"

Callum turned with a careless smile. "Nowhere in particular. Just... here. Isn't it wonderful?"

THE HEART'S MAP AND THE MIND'S COMPASS 37

Leo felt a pang of unease. He had let himself get caught up in Callum's energy, but now, with no Compass and no clear path, he was suddenly aware of how lost they truly were.

Iris glared at Callum, her face a mix of anger and frustration. "Wonderful? We're lost! There's no way back, no direction. This—this is exactly why structure matters! You can't just wander aimlessly and hope for the best."

Callum shrugged, unfazed by her outburst. "Maybe you'll find something you weren't looking for. Sometimes, being lost is the only way to truly find yourself."

As the reality of their situation settled over him, Leo felt torn. He wanted to believe in Callum's free-spirited approach, to trust that they'd stumble upon something magical. But he couldn't ignore the uneasy feeling creeping over him. Being lost here was different than following his Heart Map—it was a lack of guidance altogether, a blind plunge into uncertainty.

Iris folded her arms, glaring at Callum. "It's reckless, following nothing but intuition. Look where it's gotten us—trapped in a grove with no way out."

Callum's expression softened, and he looked at her with a mix of sympathy and understanding. "It's not about recklessness, Iris. It's about trust. Trusting the world, and trusting yourself. Not every step has to be calculated." He placed a hand over his heart. "Sometimes, the heart knows the way better than any map."

Leo watched the exchange, feeling as if he were at the center of a tug-of-war. He admired Callum's fearlessness, but Iris's words resonated with his practical side. He knew they couldn't wander forever, and the prospect of truly being lost frightened him. The Heart Map had provided guidance, a subtle but steady pull that gave him direction. Callum's approach, however, was something else entirely—an untethered journey, driven only by instinct.

Seeing the struggle on Leo's face, Callum placed a reassuring hand on his shoulder. "Don't worry, my friend. We'll find our way out of here. All you have to do is trust yourself." He looked at Iris, his gaze gentle. "And you, too, Iris. Maybe let go a little. The world won't fall apart if you take a single step without knowing exactly where it leads."

Iris sighed, her gaze softening as she looked at Leo. "Maybe... maybe he's right, Leo. Maybe there's something to be learned here, even if I don't entirely understand it." She glanced around at the grove, her rigid stance relaxing just a bit.

Leo felt a rush of relief and gratitude for both of them. Callum's unwavering faith in the journey and Iris's willingness to open her mind, even if just a little, filled him with hope. He took a deep breath, closing his eyes and allowing himself to feel the faint pulse of his Heart Map. It was faint, but it was there—an echo of guidance within the grove's wild beauty.

As they resumed their journey, Leo felt a new kind of confidence—a balance between Callum's free spirit and Iris's caution. He was still learning, still figuring out how to trust his heart without losing himself in the process. But with each step, he felt closer to understanding the delicate dance between intuition and structure, between freedom and guidance. And as they walked through the grove, he knew he was exactly where he needed to be, surrounded by friends who, despite their differences, were helping him uncover the truest parts of himself.

Chapter 7: The Cliff of Choices

The journey through the grove, with its endless stretches of wildflowers and hidden magic, lingered in Leo's mind as they finally found their way back to a more familiar path. Callum had bid them a cheerful farewell, disappearing back into the thicket of blossoms and overgrown vines, following his own uncharted course. As Leo watched him fade into the distance, he felt a pang of longing. Callum's life was untethered and boundlessly free, yet Leo had discovered the hazards of a purely heart-led journey. It was an enticing path, but also fraught with risks he wasn't sure he could embrace wholeheartedly.

Iris, now walking beside him with a renewed sense of focus, still seemed slightly uneasy from the experience, casting wary glances at the Heart Map in Leo's hands.

"He may have a point," she murmured thoughtfully. "But there's a fine line between trusting the heart and throwing caution to the wind. That grove was beautiful, but we were utterly lost. If you hadn't found the signal in your Heart Map... well, we might still be wandering."

Leo nodded, tracing his fingers over the faint, glowing lines of his Heart Map. It seemed to pulse, as if alive with a quiet energy, guiding him but never revealing too much. His journey felt more like a whisper than a shout, a gentle nudge that urged him to venture forward without fully knowing why.

"I think... maybe I need to find the balance," Leo admitted. "Callum showed me how amazing it can be to let go of control. But if I rely on my heart alone, there's no telling where I might end up."

As they continued along the rugged trail, the landscape grew wilder and more daunting. Dark green cliffs rose on either side, their rocky surfaces slick and covered in patches of moss. The forest around them thinned, replaced by jagged rocks and narrow pathways that seemed to lead nowhere. A chill wind swept through the air, stirring the leaves and sending shivers down Leo's spine.

In the distance, the path ahead suddenly dropped off into nothingness. A sharp cliff jutted out, overlooking a vast expanse of mist-shrouded valleys and mountains. The cliff path was narrow, lined with loose stones that looked as though they could crumble at the slightest touch.

"Is this... is this the only way forward?" Iris asked, her voice tight with apprehension as she eyed the precarious path.

Leo hesitated, checking his Heart Map and then glancing at the Compass, which Iris held up for guidance. The Compass pointed firmly behind them, indicating that the safer path lay in retreat. But his Heart Map was beginning to glow, the lines brightening as they faced the cliff, as if urging him to go forward.

A tug-of-war began in Leo's mind. The Heart Map pulsed, alive and insistent, almost whispering for him to take a step toward the unknown. The Compass, on the other hand, provided clear, logical guidance. To move forward would mean taking a leap of faith on a narrow, treacherous ledge. To turn back would mean safety.

"What are you thinking?" Iris asked, studying his expression. Her grip on the Compass was firm, a reminder of the steadiness it provided.

"I... I don't know," he replied honestly, still transfixed by the Heart Map. "The Heart Map wants me to keep going. But... look at this cliff. If we slip or make one wrong move, it could be disastrous."

Iris raised her eyebrows, casting a skeptical glance at the path. "Leo, the Compass is telling us to turn back. Maybe... maybe it's right this time."

But Leo felt a pull in his chest, an indescribable urge to move forward. Something within him believed that the Heart Map wasn't leading him astray, that it was guiding him toward something significant, something he wouldn't find by retreating.

"There's something out there, Iris," he said, his voice tinged with determination. "I don't know what it is, but I can feel it. I have to follow this path."

Iris stared at him, worry etched in her face. "Are you sure? Look, we've seen the dangers of following intuition without thought. The Compass... it might be the more reasonable choice."

"I know," he replied, his gaze fixed on the cliff's edge. "But I can't shake the feeling that this is important. The Heart Map has guided me this far. I need to trust it."

Iris sighed, glancing down at the Compass one more time before slipping it back into her bag. "Fine," she said, her voice resigned but supportive. "If you're sure, then I'll follow you."

With a deep breath, Leo took his first step onto the narrow path, his feet crunching against the loose stones. The cliff dropped off sharply on one side, plunging into a seemingly endless void. Every step felt like a test of his resolve, as he balanced on the thin edge, trying to keep his mind steady. He could feel his heart pounding, not just with fear, but with anticipation, with the thrill of venturing into the unknown.

Iris followed closely, her movements careful and precise. Despite her reservations, she was determined to stay by his side. Each time they reached a particularly treacherous part of the path, she glanced back, her eyes filled with the question: *Are you still sure about this?*

And each time, Leo nodded, his grip on the Heart Map steady, even though a small part of him was wrestling with doubt.

The path grew narrower as they went on, with jagged rocks jutting out from the side of the cliff. The wind howled around them, tugging at their clothes, as if testing their resolve. Every so often, a stone would slip beneath their feet, skittering down the cliffside, disappearing into the mist below. Each time it happened, Leo felt his heart skip a beat, but he kept moving forward, determined to see where the Heart Map would lead him.

As they climbed higher, the air grew thinner and colder. Leo's breath came in short gasps, but he could feel the Heart Map pulsing in his hand, its glow bright and steady, urging him forward. The Compass, now hidden in Iris's bag, felt like a distant memory, a whisper of safety that he had chosen to ignore.

They reached a point where the path became so narrow that only one of them could pass at a time. Leo went first, hugging the cliffside as he edged along, his eyes focused on the ground beneath him, trying to ignore the dizzying drop to his left. He could hear Iris's footsteps behind him, slow and careful, her breathing tense.

Just as he thought they'd made it past the narrowest part, his foot slipped on a loose rock. He stumbled, his arms flailing for balance, as he teetered on the edge. Panic shot through him, and for a brief, terrifying moment, he thought he would fall.

But then he felt a steadying hand on his shoulder. Iris had reached out, her grip firm and reassuring, pulling him back to safety.

"Leo," she said, her voice low and filled with concern. "Are you absolutely sure about this?"

Leo looked down at the Heart Map, still glowing in his hand. He felt its warmth, its gentle encouragement. Despite the fear gripping his heart, he couldn't bring himself to turn back. He took a deep breath, nodding.

"I am," he replied, his voice steadier than he felt. "I know it's risky, but... I believe there's something at the end of this path. Something worth seeing."

Iris looked at him for a long moment, her eyes searching his face. Finally, she nodded, her expression softening. "Then I'll trust you. Just... be careful."

With Iris's support, Leo felt a renewed sense of determination. Together, they continued along the cliff path, each step feeling like a triumph over fear. The Heart Map's glow grew brighter as they went on, illuminating the path ahead, guiding them through the darkness and uncertainty.

After what felt like hours of careful, nerve-wracking progress, they finally reached the end of the cliff path. The narrow ledge widened, giving way to a small, hidden plateau that overlooked the valley below. Leo gasped, his eyes widening at the sight before him.

The view was breathtaking. The clouds parted, revealing a sprawling landscape of rolling hills, rivers, and forests, bathed in the warm, golden light of the setting sun. It was as if they had stumbled upon a secret world, a place untouched by time or human hands.

In the center of the plateau stood a massive stone archway, weathered and ancient, covered in intricate carvings that seemed to shimmer in the sunlight. Leo felt drawn to it, a sense of awe filling him as he approached.

Iris followed, her eyes wide with wonder. "This... this is incredible," she whispered. "I've never seen anything like it."

Leo nodded, his heart swelling with a sense of accomplishment. He had trusted the Heart Map, even when logic told him to turn back, and it had led him to something extraordinary. This place felt sacred, as if it held secrets waiting to be uncovered.

He approached the archway, running his fingers over the carvings. They depicted scenes of journeys, of people venturing into unknown lands, guided by the stars and their hearts. It was a testament to the courage of those who had come before him, those who had chosen the path of the heart over the path of logic.

For the first time, Leo felt a deep sense of clarity. He understood now that following the heart wasn't about ignoring logic; it was about balancing it with intuition, about trusting oneself even in the face of fear.

As they sat on the plateau, taking in the view, Leo reflected on the journey that had brought them here. He had faced his fears, made difficult choices, and learned to trust his heart in ways he never thought possible.

"I think... I think I finally understand," he said, turning to Iris. "The heart's path isn't about recklessness. It's about faith. About believing in something even when you can't see it."

Iris smiled, her expression softening. "Maybe you're right. Maybe there's more to life than just following a strict path. Sometimes, the heart knows things the mind can't explain."

They sat in silence, letting the beauty of the moment sink in. Leo knew that he would carry this experience with him, that it had changed him in ways he couldn't yet fully comprehend. The cliff of choices had tested him, challenged him, but it had also revealed the strength within him to face the unknown.

As they made their way back down the path, Leo felt a new sense of confidence, a balance between logic and intuition that he would carry with him on the rest of his journey. The Heart Map pulsed gently in his hand, a reminder of the choices he had made and the path he had chosen.

In the end, he had followed his heart, and it had led him to a place of wonder, a place he would never have found if he had turned back. And as he walked away from the cliff of choices, he knew that this was just the beginning of the discoveries that awaited him.

Chapter 8: Solon the Wanderer

As Leo and Iris made their way back down from the cliff plateau, the descent seemed somehow different from the ascent. Though the path was equally narrow, Leo felt lighter, as if the discovery at the cliff's end had unlocked something within him. He was starting to see that there was a way to balance the two forces that had been tugging him in opposite directions—the unyielding clarity of the Compass and the mysterious allure of his Heart Map.

But he still had questions, ones he didn't yet know how to answer. When they finally reached a safer stretch of ground, a part of him felt relieved, but another part missed the thrill of walking that fine line. Just as he was trying to wrap his mind around this strange inner tug-of-war, a figure appeared up ahead, traveling the same path toward them.

He was an older man, though his stride was steady and strong. His face was lined with the marks of experience, and his dark, sun-weathered skin was offset by a gentle, curious expression in his eyes. He wore a simple traveler's cloak, tattered at the edges, and a leather satchel hung at his side. His Compass dangled from a cord around his neck, and in his hand, he held a Heart Map, carefully folded and well-worn.

As the man approached, he smiled, a warm, knowing smile that suggested he had been expecting them.

"Greetings, travelers," he said in a voice deep and resonant. "You must be on quite a journey to have ventured to the Cliff of Choices. Not many make it that far."

Leo and Iris exchanged glances, surprised by the man's ease and familiarity.

"Hello," Leo replied, feeling a bit self-conscious. "Yes, we're... we're following this Heart Map. It led us to the cliff, but we weren't sure if we were doing the right thing."

The man chuckled, a sound rich with amusement and wisdom. "Ah, the Heart Map. A curious tool, isn't it? Always nudging you toward places you'd never think to go. And yet, it's never entirely clear why."

"I'm trying to understand it," Leo continued. "Sometimes it feels right, like it's showing me where I need to go. Other times... well, I feel like I'm stumbling in the dark."

The man nodded thoughtfully. "It sounds like you've met the joys and the challenges of following the heart. But I believe it's time for you to learn about balance."

Leo leaned in, intrigued. "Are you saying you know how to use both? The Compass and the Heart Map?"

The man gave a wry smile, his eyes twinkling. "Indeed. My name is Solon, and I've spent years traveling these lands, learning the ways of both logic and intuition. If you're willing, I can share what I've learned with you."

The three of them settled on a large flat rock, with Iris and Leo listening intently as Solon began his tale.

"Like you, Leo, I started with a Heart Map," Solon began. "I was young, adventurous, and a bit foolish. My Heart Map led me to places I never would have gone otherwise—places of beauty, yes, but also places of danger. There were times I felt exhilarated, alive, as if the Heart Map had shown me the true essence of life. But there were also times it led me astray, leaving me stranded, lost, and questioning my choices."

He paused, glancing down at his own Heart Map, worn and faded. "I learned the hard way that the heart, while powerful, cannot guide you alone. There were things I missed, opportunities and safety nets that the Compass could have shown me had I only been open to it."

Iris nodded, her gaze unwavering. "So what did you do?"

THE HEART'S MAP AND THE MIND'S COMPASS

"I learned to respect both," Solon replied. "When I finally found a Compass, I saw how much easier it made my travels. It pointed out safe routes, gave me direction when I felt lost, and helped me avoid pitfalls. But after a time, I began to rely on it too much. I became cautious, careful, and less willing to explore. My journey grew safe, but it also grew dull. I realized that the Compass, for all its precision, could never lead me to the extraordinary places the Heart Map had shown me."

"So... you found a balance?" Leo asked, his eyes filled with wonder.

"Exactly," Solon said. "It wasn't easy, and it took me years to figure out. But I learned that both tools have their own wisdom, their own value. I began to consult both, letting them work together rather than pulling me in separate directions."

Solon reached into his satchel and pulled out his Heart Map, spreading it out for Leo and Iris to see. Its lines were faint but steady, forming intricate patterns that branched out in all directions, as if inviting him to explore countless possibilities. Then he held up his Compass, letting it catch the light. The needle quivered slightly, pointing steadfastly in a single direction.

"What I came to understand," Solon said, "is that the Heart Map and the Compass each represent different aspects of ourselves. The Heart Map is our intuition, our dreams, our curiosity. It leads us toward growth, beauty, and wonder. The Compass, on the other hand, represents logic, safety, and experience. It grounds us, keeps us safe, and ensures we stay on solid ground."

Leo leaned closer, mesmerized. "But how do you know when to trust one over the other?"

Solon smiled. "That is the essence of balance. It requires practice and patience. The first step is to listen to both without judgment. When you look at the path ahead, consult both tools and see where they align and where they diverge."

Leo's mind raced as he absorbed Solon's words. "Can you show us? I want to know how you make your choices."

"Of course," Solon replied, nodding. "Let's try a simple exercise. Picture a fork in the road up ahead. One path is the familiar, safe route; the other is unknown, perhaps even a bit risky."

Leo closed his eyes, letting the imaginary paths form in his mind. He could almost feel the pull of the Compass toward the familiar path, while the Heart Map urged him down the unexplored one.

"When you open your eyes, imagine holding both tools and asking yourself: What do I value most right now? Safety or adventure? Stability or discovery? Sometimes, the answer lies within you rather than in the tools themselves."

Leo's eyes opened, and he took a deep breath. He thought of the narrow cliff path he and Iris had braved, of the exhilaration he'd felt in the unknown, tempered by the thrill of finding something valuable. "So... sometimes it's about knowing what you're ready for?"

"Exactly," Solon said, smiling. "Balance is about being attuned to yourself as much as to the world around you."

As they walked further, Solon led Leo and Iris to another cliff, though this one was less daunting than the previous one. It overlooked a small valley dotted with vibrant wildflowers and crisscrossed by streams.

"There's a trail here," Solon said, pointing down the side of the cliff, where a faint, winding path disappeared into the valley. "It's not particularly dangerous, but it can be tricky in spots. The Compass suggests taking the longer, easier route around the cliff. The Heart Map, however, is eager for us to go down this path."

Leo felt the familiar thrill of adventure mixed with a touch of apprehension. He could see the beauty waiting below, but he also knew that the path would require careful footing.

"What do you think, Leo?" Solon asked, watching him closely.

Leo hesitated, holding both the Heart Map and the Compass in his hands. He could feel each tool pulling him in a different direction, but this time, he took a moment to consider his own feelings, his own readiness.

"I think... I think I'd like to try the valley path," he said finally. "But I'll go slowly, taking each step carefully. That way, I can have the adventure without putting myself or Iris in too much danger."

Solon's eyes sparkled with approval. "Well said, Leo. That's the essence of balance—choosing the path that calls to you, but with a mindful approach."

As they descended the cliff, Leo found himself following Solon's example, pausing at each tricky spot to check his footing, feeling the thrill of discovery tempered by a newfound caution. He was starting to see that balance wasn't about denying one path or the other; it was about learning to navigate both, letting them enrich each other.

They spent the next few hours exploring the valley, guided by Solon's steady wisdom. He taught them to look for subtle signs—birds taking flight, the sound of rustling leaves, the feel of the earth beneath their feet—that could offer clues about the path ahead.

As they walked, Solon shared stories of his travels, tales of places both beautiful and treacherous, and the people he'd met along the way. Each story carried a lesson, a nugget of wisdom that he had learned through experience.

"The greatest journey, Leo, is the one that teaches you to trust yourself," Solon said as they rested by a stream. "The tools are guides, yes, but in the end, it's your heart and mind that must work together."

Leo nodded, feeling the weight of Solon's words. He was beginning to understand that the Compass and the Heart Map were extensions of his own instincts, tools that could guide him but would never replace his own judgment.

As they prepared to part ways, Solon turned to Leo, his expression serious but warm. "Remember, Leo, balance is not a destination; it's a practice. Every day, every step, you will face choices that require you to listen to both the heart and the mind. Trust yourself to know when to follow one, the other, or perhaps both."

Leo watched as Solon disappeared down a different path, feeling both grateful and humbled by the encounter. The man's wisdom had touched something deep within him, awakening a sense of confidence and clarity he hadn't known he possessed.

"I think we're ready," Leo said to Iris, holding up both the Heart Map and the Compass. "Ready to keep going, with both tools guiding us."

As they walked away from the valley, Leo felt a sense of peace, a quiet assurance that he was finally learning to trust himself. His journey would still be filled with challenges, choices, and unknowns, but he knew now that he could face them with balance, drawing strength from both his heart and his mind.

For the first time in his life, Leo felt whole. And as he and Iris continued down the path, he realized that the real journey was just beginning—the journey of discovering who he truly was, and the wisdom that lay within.

Chapter 9: The Valley of Reflections

As the sun dipped toward the horizon, casting a warm amber glow over the mountains, Solon led Leo and Iris down a sloping path into a valley that seemed to shimmer with an almost ethereal light. There was a stillness in the air, a hushed silence that made every step feel profound, as if they were approaching a sacred space.

"This is the Valley of Reflections," Solon said, his voice softer than usual, almost reverent. "Many travelers pass through here, but few are truly prepared for what they encounter."

Leo and Iris exchanged glances, their curiosity piqued and nerves tingling. The valley stretched out before them, blanketed in tall, silvery grass that swayed gently with the evening breeze. Small streams crisscrossed through the grass, their waters crystal clear, and as Leo looked closer, he realized he could see his own reflection staring back up at him.

"What happens here?" Iris asked, her tone cautious but intrigued.

"In this valley," Solon explained, "each person must confront their own inner self, their hidden fears and desires, as if looking into a mirror. It is a place where truth emerges—not the easy, surface truth, but the truth within, the parts of ourselves we often ignore."

Leo's pulse quickened. He had encountered challenges of both mind and heart on this journey, but nothing had felt as personal as what Solon was describing.

"You mean... we'll see parts of ourselves we don't usually see?" Leo asked, his voice barely more than a whisper.

Solon nodded. "Exactly. This valley will show you the extremes of your nature—what it looks like to live solely by logic and then solely by emotion. It can be unsettling, even difficult, but if you're willing, you may discover a balance that lies beyond either extreme."

Taking a steadying breath, Leo stepped forward, feeling a strange blend of anticipation and apprehension. He knew this was an essential step in his journey, a trial he had to face alone.

As Leo ventured further into the valley, he noticed a patch of earth beside one of the streams that seemed to shimmer differently. He knelt beside it and peered down into the water. His own reflection looked back at him, but then, as he gazed more intently, the image began to shift.

He saw himself in an unfamiliar scene—a world of order and precision. He was standing in a vast, spotless hall filled with rows of books and maps. His clothes were crisp and formal, and in his hand, he held a Compass, its needle unwavering as it pointed in a single, resolute direction.

This vision of himself seemed calm, collected, and entirely composed. He moved with purpose, his every action methodical and efficient. Leo could feel the sense of certainty that radiated from this version of himself, as if he had absolute control over every aspect of his life.

As he watched, Leo saw this logical version of himself interact with others in a distant, calculated way. Every conversation was measured, every decision weighed for its practical value. Emotions were subdued, kept firmly in check, and intuition was dismissed as unreliable. This Leo had found a comfort zone in structure, in rules and plans, where everything had a purpose and a place.

At first, the vision felt reassuring. After all, he often wished for this kind of clarity and control. But as he observed more closely, he began to notice the cost of such a rigid approach. This version of himself was isolated, detached from the spontaneity and joy that he often found in moments of genuine connection. His relationships seemed shallow, transactional even, as if people were just another factor in his carefully calculated life.

Leo felt a pang of sadness as he watched himself in this logical life. Yes, this version of himself was successful and respected, but he seemed devoid of warmth, of passion. There was no spark of wonder, no thrill of discovery. His days were predictable, unchanging, and, ultimately, empty.

Leo shook his head, stepping back from the reflection in the water. As he took a deep breath, the image shifted, giving way to a new vision, one that filled him with both curiosity and trepidation.

In this new scene, he saw himself surrounded by people, his eyes alight with excitement. This version of himself was animated, expressive, and vibrant, his face an open canvas for every passing emotion. He held the Heart Map tightly, almost reverently, and seemed to follow its guidance with an unshakable trust.

This Leo was immersed in his emotions, allowing them to guide every step he took. He embraced joy, sorrow, and every feeling in between without restraint, his heart open to the world and all its experiences. The world around him was colorful, full of music, laughter, and spontaneity.

But as he watched, Leo saw that this life, too, had its pitfalls. While this version of himself was passionate and lively, he also appeared lost, drifting aimlessly from one impulse to the next. He would throw himself into projects, relationships, and adventures with enthusiasm, only to abandon them when his interest waned or his feelings shifted. He seemed unable to commit, to hold steady on any single path.

Leo noticed the subtle toll this lifestyle took on those around him. Friends and loved ones looked weary, confused, uncertain of his intentions. His relationships were intense but fleeting, filled with passion but lacking stability. There was beauty in this life of pure emotion, yes, but there was also chaos, instability, and, at times, a lingering sense of loneliness.

For a moment, Leo felt drawn to the excitement of this life, the freedom of following his heart wherever it led. But he also saw the exhaustion, the perpetual restlessness, and the way this version of himself seemed to lack direction. There was a beauty here, but it was as fleeting as it was vivid.

Leo stepped back from the reflection, feeling a swirl of conflicting emotions within him. He had seen two extremes—one driven by pure logic, the other by unrestrained emotion. Each had its allure, but each also had its limitations, its sacrifices.

He felt the weight of his own choices, the tension between his Compass and Heart Map, more keenly than ever. It was as if two parts of himself were pulling him in opposite directions, each one convinced it was the right way.

"What do I do?" he whispered, his voice barely audible in the silence of the valley.

He sank to the ground, closing his eyes, and let the images of both lives wash over him. The logical life and the emotional life each held something he valued, something essential. But he knew now that choosing one over the other would mean losing a part of himself.

As he sat in quiet reflection, he felt a calmness settle over him, a realization that perhaps he didn't have to choose between the two. He remembered Solon's words: "Balance is not a destination; it's a practice." Maybe the answer wasn't in picking one path but in learning to walk between them, to find a middle ground that honored both his logic and his emotions.

With this newfound insight, Leo returned to the stream, gazing once more into its depths. This time, his reflection was different. He saw himself as he was now, holding both the Compass and the Heart Map in his hands. The Compass pointed steadily, guiding him forward with purpose, while the Heart Map pulsed softly, illuminating paths he hadn't yet considered.

In this vision, Leo was not a slave to logic or emotion. Instead, he saw himself blending both, allowing each tool to inform his choices without letting either dominate. He saw himself making decisions that were guided by both his head and his heart, moving forward with clarity and courage.

This version of himself looked stronger, more assured, and somehow more complete. There was a warmth in his eyes, a steadiness in his stance, and a quiet confidence that came from knowing he could navigate life's twists and turns with both intelligence and passion.

When he finally tore himself away from the reflection, he found Iris waiting nearby, watching him with a knowing look.

"What did you see?" she asked softly.

Leo took a deep breath, choosing his words carefully. "I saw... two versions of myself. One who relied only on logic, and one who lived by pure emotion. They were both parts of me, but they were... incomplete."

Iris nodded, her expression thoughtful. "And which one do you think is the real you?"

Leo paused, the answer forming slowly in his mind. "I think... I think I'm both. I need my Compass to guide me, to keep me grounded, but I also need my Heart Map to push me to places I wouldn't go otherwise. It's not about choosing one over the other; it's about letting them work together."

A smile spread across Iris's face, a smile of understanding and approval. "It sounds like you've found your answer."

Leo felt a surge of relief, as if a weight had been lifted from his shoulders. He had spent so much time wrestling with the question of which tool to trust, which path to follow. But now, he saw that he didn't have to choose one over the other. He could carry both, letting each one guide him in its own way.

As they left the Valley of Reflections, Leo felt a newfound sense of clarity and purpose. He knew the journey ahead would still be filled with challenges, moments where he would question himself and his path. But he also knew that he had the tools he needed to face those challenges with both wisdom and courage.

The Valley of Reflections had shown him his inner conflict, but it had also given him the strength to move beyond it, to embrace a balance that honored both his head and his heart. For the first time, Leo felt like he was truly ready for whatever lay ahead.

As he and Iris continued down the path, the sun dipping below the horizon, Leo carried with him a sense of peace and confidence. The journey was far from over, but he was no longer afraid. He was ready to face whatever came next, with both his Compass and Heart Map guiding him, side by side.

Chapter 10: The Hidden Glade

The path twisted and turned, winding deeper into the thick forest, and with each step, the air grew more fragrant and the colors around Leo and Iris seemed richer, more alive. Flowers in vibrant hues dotted the underbrush, and sunlight filtered through the canopy in dappled patterns that painted the ground in gold. This place felt enchanted, as though each leaf and stone held secrets waiting to be discovered.

Leo looked down at the Heart Map, which pulsed softly, its glow warm and reassuring. It had been a constant guide, showing him paths his logical mind might have dismissed. But now, something about the glowing trails felt different, more intricate. The map didn't point in a single direction but instead revealed multiple paths, each one shimmering with a slightly different hue.

Iris leaned over his shoulder, her brow furrowed in curiosity. "It seems like it's leading us... everywhere?" she said, her tone a mixture of wonder and concern.

"Yes," Leo replied, feeling a strange mix of excitement and trepidation. "It's as if each path has its own purpose, its own story. This place must be... the Lost Glade."

Solon had spoken of this legendary place, a hidden part of the forest that very few travelers ever found. It was said to be a place of beauty and mystery, but also of trials. Those who entered the Glade had to learn to trust both heart and mind, or risk getting lost within its enchanting, ever-shifting paths.

As he took his first steps forward, Leo felt the weight of the Heart Map and the Compass pressing against him, each one drawing him in slightly different directions. It was clear that neither tool alone could guide him safely through the Glade. He would have to find a way to balance them.

The first path the Heart Map illuminated was a narrow, winding trail lined with silver-leaved trees and dotted with wildflowers. The flowers emitted a soft glow, their luminescence growing stronger as Leo and Iris approached. The trail had an inviting quality, like it was calling them toward something thrilling and extraordinary.

"This feels... magical," Iris whispered, her eyes wide with wonder. "Should we take it?"

Leo looked down at the Compass, which pointed firmly to the right, away from the glowing trail. It was a clear sign: logic told him this path was risky, potentially leading them away from their destination. But the Heart Map pulsed with encouragement, as if urging him to take a leap of faith.

After a moment of consideration, Leo decided to follow the Heart Map, trusting that there was something valuable to be learned on this trail. They made their way forward, each step feeling more exhilarating than the last. The path led them through thickets of shimmering vines and under arches of ivy, until finally, they emerged into a small clearing where a waterfall cascaded into a crystal-clear pool.

"This is incredible!" Leo exclaimed, his heart swelling with a sense of wonder and gratitude.

But as he marveled at the scene, he realized they had reached a dead end. There was no exit from the clearing, no continuation of the path. They had wandered off course, guided by curiosity but now faced with the reality that this detour had taken them nowhere.

Leo felt a pang of frustration. He had followed his heart, trusting the allure of the glowing flowers and the enchanting scene, but it had led him astray.

"I think this was a lesson," he said, glancing at Iris. "The Heart Map brought us here to show us the beauty of the journey, but without a clear destination, we were just... wandering."

"Maybe that's the point," Iris suggested. "Sometimes the heart takes us to places that might seem pointless but are beautiful experiences in their own right. We just have to know when to keep going and when to pull back."

Nodding, Leo consulted the Compass, which pointed them back the way they came. He resolved to use both tools, letting his heart guide him toward experiences while relying on his mind to keep him grounded.

Back at the crossroads, Leo studied the Heart Map again. Another trail shimmered to their left, winding through dense thickets of brambles and thorn-covered bushes. This path looked less inviting, even foreboding, but the Heart Map pulsed with a steady, gentle glow, urging him to explore despite the obstacles.

"I don't know, Leo," Iris said, eyeing the path with apprehension. "Are you sure about this one?"

The Compass pointed once more toward a safer, clearer trail nearby, a direction that promised easier passage. But Leo remembered his vow to find balance. He decided to heed the Heart Map, knowing that sometimes the heart led to challenges that could reveal hidden strengths.

They stepped onto the path, moving slowly to avoid the prickly brambles that reached out like fingers, snagging at their clothes. The thorns caught on Leo's sleeves, tearing small holes in the fabric, but he pressed on, his determination fueled by an intuition that there was something important ahead.

At last, they emerged into a glade filled with strange, twisted trees. Among them stood an enormous, ancient oak, its trunk thick and gnarled, with carvings that spiraled up its bark. Each carving seemed to tell a story—of travelers before them, of struggles and triumphs, of love and loss. The sight was both haunting and beautiful, a testament to the endurance of those who had walked the path before him.

"This feels... significant," Leo murmured, running his hand over the carvings. He could feel the energy of the place, the weight of countless stories etched into the bark.

"Maybe it's telling us that there's value in hardship," Iris suggested, her fingers tracing one of the intricate carvings. "That facing difficulty leaves a mark, a kind of legacy."

Leo nodded, realizing that without the thorns and the struggle to reach this place, they might not have fully appreciated the significance of the tree and its carvings. This path had required caution and perseverance, but it had led to something meaningful.

Consulting the Compass once more, he found that it pointed forward now, aligned with the Heart Map. For the first time, the two tools were guiding him in harmony, and he felt a deep sense of satisfaction. He was learning to navigate not just with his heart or his mind, but with both.

Continuing along the path, Leo and Iris finally arrived at a hidden pond nestled in the heart of the Glade. Its surface was so smooth and clear that it looked like a mirror, reflecting the sky, trees, and even their own faces with perfect clarity. The pond's reflection was mesmerizing, almost hypnotic, as though it held the secrets of the world within its depths.

The Heart Map pulsed brighter than ever, illuminating the path to the pond's edge, while the Compass pointed slightly away, indicating a path that skirted around it. Leo felt a pang of hesitation, caught between the allure of the Heart Map and the caution of the Compass.

"It's like the Compass is warning us," Iris observed, glancing between the tools and the pond. "Maybe it's telling us to be careful, to avoid diving too deep."

Leo nodded, feeling the tension between the two tools. He knew the Heart Map wanted him to confront something here, but the Compass was urging caution, reminding him not to be reckless. Balancing his curiosity with his logical mind, he decided to kneel beside the pond instead of stepping into it.

As he peered into the water, Leo saw his reflection change, much like it had in the Valley of Reflections. This time, however, he saw not just his logical or emotional self, but a synthesis of the two. He saw himself consulting both tools, making choices that were both courageous and wise, and he realized that this version of himself was stronger, more complete.

He saw visions of himself facing future challenges, some that would require swift, heart-led decisions and others that would demand patience and caution. He saw himself learning, growing, and becoming more attuned to the delicate dance between his head and heart.

"It's like the pond is showing us what we can become," he murmured, awed by the clarity of the vision.

Iris leaned over, looking at her own reflection. "I think it's a reminder that we have everything we need within us," she said softly. "We just have to learn to use it wisely."

They spent a long time by the pond, contemplating the reflections and the lessons they had learned in the Glade. Each experience—the path of adventure, the path of caution, and the pond of self-reflection—had revealed different aspects of balance, showing Leo how to trust both his Compass and Heart Map in harmony.

As they made their way out of the Hidden Glade, Leo felt a profound sense of peace. He knew now that he didn't have to choose between his head and heart. He could walk a path that honored both, allowing each tool to guide him in different ways.

The Compass would keep him grounded, helping him make practical decisions and avoid unnecessary risks, while the Heart Map would lead him toward experiences that enriched his soul and brought depth to his journey.

Iris walked beside him, her expression thoughtful. "This journey has been more than just a way forward, hasn't it?" she said. "It's been about learning who we are, what we truly need."

Leo nodded, feeling the weight of her words. The Hidden Glade had given him more than directions—it had given him insight, courage, and a sense of purpose that went beyond any destination.

As they left the Glade, the Heart Map and Compass lay peacefully in his hands, their energies no longer in conflict but in harmony. Leo understood that this balance was a skill he would have to nurture, a constant journey rather than a final destination.

But for the first time, he felt ready. With his head and heart aligned, he knew he could face whatever challenges lay ahead, carrying forward the wisdom he had gained in the Glade and beyond.

Chapter 11: The Crystal of Balance

Leo and Iris continued through the heart of the Lost Glade, the dense forest clearing little by little to reveal a sight unlike anything they had ever seen. It was as if they were walking through an ancient and sacred place, a space that had waited quietly for generations, revealing itself only to those prepared to understand its mysteries.

The trees parted to reveal a circular clearing bathed in an otherworldly light. In the center of the clearing, perched on a raised stone pedestal, was a massive crystal—clear and pristine, yet shimmering with a spectrum of colors that danced across its facets like beams of trapped starlight. Leo's Heart Map pulsed in harmony with the crystal, almost as though it recognized the artifact's significance.

"This must be the Crystal of Balance," Iris whispered in awe, her eyes wide as she gazed at the radiant gem. She had heard legends of such a crystal but had always assumed it was just a myth.

Leo stepped forward, his heart racing with a mixture of anticipation and reverence. He knew he hadn't reached this place by chance; his journey through the trials of the Glade had been a preparation for this very moment. The Crystal seemed to hum softly, its resonance vibrating through him, as if it could sense his arrival and his purpose.

"Solon spoke of this," Leo said quietly, recalling the wise words of the old wanderer who had guided them. "He said that only those willing to seek true balance would ever find it."

As he reached out to touch the crystal, a sudden flash of light enveloped him. Leo's vision blurred, and he felt as though he was being pulled into the very heart of the crystal, into a realm where time and space blended together, showing him truths that lay beyond his everyday understanding.

The light faded, and Leo found himself standing in the middle of his village. He recognized familiar faces around him—people he had grown up with, friends and neighbors he had known all his life. Yet something was different; the village looked more muted, its colors less vibrant, as though it was a shadow of itself.

In front of him, he saw old Master Eamon, a wise elder of the village known for his strict adherence to the Compass. He was renowned for his discipline and logical mind, a figure whom many villagers looked up to. Eamon moved through the village with precision, each step calculated, each task meticulously planned. Yet, as Leo observed him more closely, he noticed an emptiness in the man's eyes, a hint of restlessness that seemed to contradict his calm, ordered life.

Eamon greeted his neighbors with polite nods but never lingered, never laughed freely or shared a warm story. He had mastered his Compass, letting it guide him unerringly through every aspect of his life, but in doing so, he had closed himself off to spontaneity, to the joy that came from following the heart's unpredictable paths.

As Leo watched, he saw Eamon refuse an invitation to join a village celebration, explaining with logic and reason why his responsibilities were more important than revelry. The villagers accepted his response with respect, but Leo could see the missed connections, the lost moments that could have enriched Eamon's life in ways beyond productivity.

A deep sense of sadness washed over Leo. He realized that Eamon had a full life in the practical sense, yet his soul seemed malnourished, his heart closed to the experiences that brought color and depth to existence.

The scene shifted, and now Leo saw Sari, a cheerful young woman known for her vibrant spirit and her deep connection to her Heart Map. Sari was a free soul, unrestrained by the bounds of routine or planning. She moved through the village like a gust of wind, her laughter echoing in the air as she followed her impulses, her Heart Map shining brightly as it guided her from one adventure to the next.

But as Leo watched her, he began to notice the chaos that followed in her wake. She would start projects with great enthusiasm, only to abandon them halfway through when her Heart Map led her elsewhere. She constantly sought the next thrill, the next new experience, but rarely lingered long enough to build anything lasting. Sari's life was a kaleidoscope of colors, each one dazzling and intense, but fleeting.

He saw villagers relying on her for tasks she'd eagerly volunteered to do, only to be left disappointed when her enthusiasm waned. She moved like a spark, lighting up lives momentarily but never remaining long enough to forge bonds of true meaning. Her spontaneity and passion were beautiful, but they lacked the grounding needed to create stability or trust.

For the first time, Leo understood the limits of a heart-led life. Sari's world was rich in emotion and experience, but it lacked the structure that would allow her to build something lasting and meaningful.

The visions faded, and Leo found himself standing before the Crystal of Balance once more. He could feel the weight of what he had witnessed pressing down on him, the emptiness of a life led solely by the Compass and the chaos of a life guided only by the Heart Map. He understood now that each path, when followed in isolation, led to an incomplete life.

But then, the Crystal began to show him something new—images of villagers who had learned to blend the two. He saw a family building a home, carefully planning each detail while also allowing for moments of spontaneous joy and celebration. He saw friends working together on projects, balancing their desire for creative expression with a commitment to seeing their work through.

He saw people who used their Compass to guide them toward stability and their Heart Map to infuse their lives with passion and adventure. These were lives lived in harmony, each day a blend of purpose and joy, of reason and wonder. He could see that these people were neither bound nor aimless but walked paths rich in both meaning and fulfillment.

The Crystal's message was clear: true wisdom lay in the ability to draw from both sources, to use the Compass for structure and direction while allowing the Heart Map to bring beauty, courage, and connection. Balance was not a static state but a dynamic dance, a willingness to listen to both the head and heart.

As Leo pondered the lesson, the Crystal glowed brighter, enveloping him in a light that felt warm and reassuring, like an embrace from an old friend. He understood now that he had been given these tools for a reason; they were not meant to be chosen between but used together.

He thought back on his journey, on the trials he had faced in the Glade, each one teaching him a different aspect of balance. The paths that led nowhere, the reflections in the Mirror Pond, and even the lessons from Solon and the villagers had all prepared him for this moment. He had to learn that his head and heart were not rivals but allies.

Leo reached out, placing both the Compass and the Heart Map on the pedestal beside the Crystal. As he did, the three objects seemed to resonate together, each one glowing in harmony with the others. The crystal's light reflected in the Compass, casting soft beams that pointed in all directions, while the Heart Map pulsed gently, its pathways intertwining with those of the Compass.

This fusion of energies was a revelation—an understanding that neither tool was complete without the other. The Compass provided direction and discipline, while the Heart Map gave purpose and

THE HEART'S MAP AND THE MIND'S COMPASS 67

emotion. Each was a vital part of the whole, and only by honoring both could he hope to live a balanced, fulfilled life.

When the vision faded, Leo felt a deep sense of calm. The lessons of the Crystal had seeped into his very being, transforming his understanding of himself and his purpose. He no longer felt the need to choose between the Compass and the Heart Map, for he knew now that they were both integral parts of his journey.

Turning to Iris, he found her watching him with a mixture of awe and understanding. She had been by his side through every trial, witnessing his growth and his struggles.

"I think... I finally understand," Leo said, his voice soft but resolute. "It's not about choosing between the Compass or the Heart Map. It's about knowing when to let each one lead, about letting them work together."

Iris smiled, nodding. "It seems simple, but finding that balance is one of the hardest things any of us can do. You've come a long way, Leo."

He smiled back, feeling a new sense of gratitude for her companionship and for the challenges that had shaped him. They stood before the Crystal, basking in its glow, knowing that their journey was far from over but that they were prepared for whatever lay ahead.

As they turned to leave the Lost Glade, Leo carried with him the wisdom of the Crystal, the courage to trust his heart, and the discipline to follow his mind. He knew there would be more trials to come, more choices to make, but he was ready. The Compass and the Heart Map rested peacefully in his hands, their energies united in harmony—a symbol of his newfound understanding of balance.

In his heart, Leo made a promise to himself: to honor both his head and heart, to listen to the wisdom of each and to trust that by doing so, he would walk a path rich with purpose, beauty, and fulfillment.

With a final glance at the Crystal of Balance, Leo and Iris stepped forward, leaving the Glade with a newfound sense of peace and a deeper connection to the wisdom that lay within them. They had found not only a mythical artifact but a timeless truth—a guide to navigating the twists and turns of life with both clarity and courage.

Chapter 12: The Journey Back

As the first rays of sunlight touched the Lost Glade, Leo and Iris prepared to leave, their hearts fuller and their minds clearer than when they first embarked on this journey. Leo glanced at the Compass and Heart Map in his hands, each now feeling like an extension of himself rather than separate, conflicting tools. The Crystal of Balance had done more than reveal wisdom; it had transformed him. He knew that the path home would be different, not just because he was different, but because he wanted to share what he'd learned.

He looked around at Iris and Callum, who had chosen to stay by his side even through the challenges. Callum, the wandering musician with a carefree spirit, had been curious about the journey, his eyes constantly on the open sky, eager to follow wherever his heart led him. And Iris, thoughtful and cautious, had brought balance to Callum's spontaneity, yet had her own journey of opening up to the wisdom of the heart. Together, they formed a group with a shared purpose—to find balance in their own lives and bring this newfound understanding back to their village.

The trek back was initially filled with lighthearted conversation and laughter, a stark contrast to the silent intensity of their journey to the Glade. Yet Leo noticed that each time they reached a fork or a choice, old habits resurfaced. Callum would start down one path impulsively, only to pause when Iris pointed out the practicality of another. They would look to Leo, who took his time, glancing between his Compass and his Heart Map, allowing both tools to weigh in before making a decision.

One afternoon, they came across a long, winding forest trail on one side and a steep shortcut on the other. Callum's instinct was immediate.

"Let's go up! It's faster and way more exciting!" he said with a mischievous grin, his gaze already fixed on the shortcut.

Leo held up a hand, gently urging him to pause. "Sometimes the faster path isn't the better one. Let's take a moment to consider both."

Callum sighed, clearly restless, but Iris looked at Leo with understanding. She watched as he examined the Heart Map, noting the path's energetic feel, its intrigue and excitement. Then he checked the Compass, which indicated stability in the winding forest trail.

"Sometimes, a journey isn't about getting somewhere fast, Callum," Leo explained, his tone calm but firm. "If we rush, we might miss something important along the way. We're going home, but we're also here to learn, to experience. The Compass suggests that the forest trail is safer and steady. But the Heart Map shows me that the shortcut has its own value—adventure and spontaneity. We need to balance the two."

Callum nodded slowly, beginning to understand that balance wasn't about restricting himself. It was about finding meaning in both the thrill of the unknown and the peace of consistency. Together, they chose the longer path, walking through the forest, where they came across small clearings with breathtaking views and noticed subtle signs of nature's beauty. The lessons of patience and presence became clearer with each step, reinforcing Leo's new wisdom.

As days turned into weeks, Iris found herself drawn to Leo's balanced approach. She had always relied heavily on her Compass, finding security in its structure. Yet now, inspired by Leo's growth, she began to explore the possibilities of the Heart Map. It was challenging for her, but Leo's guidance was gentle and encouraging.

One evening, as they camped by a stream, Leo decided to show Iris how to listen to the subtle whispers of her heart. He sat beside her, placing his Heart Map and Compass between them.

"I used to think I had to pick one—logic or intuition, the head or the heart," Leo began. "But I realized that when I allow both to guide me, they bring out the best in each other. I know you've always been more comfortable with the Compass. But I think the Heart Map has something valuable to show you too."

Iris looked at the Heart Map, hesitant but curious. "It feels strange to me, to trust something so... unstructured."

"Maybe think of it like a friend," Leo suggested. "Sometimes, it doesn't need to make sense immediately. Sometimes, it just needs you to listen. Start small; take a deep breath and just let your heart show you where it wants to go."

They sat in silence, and Iris allowed herself to breathe slowly, feeling the evening breeze and the rhythm of her own heartbeat. She was surprised by a gentle tug from within, a feeling that encouraged her to walk over to the stream and simply sit by its edge. For the first time, she followed this unstructured nudge, letting herself be led without analyzing it.

When she returned, her expression was soft, almost serene. "I can see why this has its own value. It doesn't give you answers; it just gives you... peace, and maybe insight that isn't always obvious."

Leo smiled, seeing how Iris was beginning to loosen her grip on control, learning to appreciate the flexibility that came from letting the heart lead sometimes. Each step she took towards balance encouraged him, reaffirming that sharing his wisdom was a path of fulfillment in itself.

The journey continued, and while Iris learned to open up to the Heart Map, Callum faced a different struggle. He was naturally free-spirited, but he often felt lost, lacking a clear direction or purpose. He admired Leo's ease with the Compass, watching as Leo combined it with his Heart Map to move confidently through uncertain terrain.

One evening, as they set up camp, Callum sat beside Leo, his usual cheerful demeanor replaced by an unusual seriousness.

"Leo, how do you follow something as rigid as a Compass without feeling like you're caging yourself?" he asked, his gaze distant.

Leo pondered this for a moment, understanding Callum's struggle. "The Compass isn't about restriction; it's about giving you stability. Think of it like a foundation. It keeps you grounded, so when you do follow your Heart Map, you have a sense of purpose and direction. Without it, you might find yourself going in circles."

Callum nodded thoughtfully. "I suppose I've always been so afraid of being stuck that I never thought of structure as something that could free me."

Leo placed his hand on Callum's shoulder. "You're not losing your freedom by having direction. You're enhancing it. The Compass doesn't limit your heart; it empowers it. With a stable foundation, you can reach higher and dream bigger because you know you have something to rely on."

Over the next few days, Leo guided Callum in small exercises, showing him how to use the Compass to find a grounded purpose while still embracing the freedom of his Heart Map. Slowly, Callum began to understand that direction didn't confine him; it supported him, enabling him to reach greater heights in his explorations and passions.

As the trio neared the village, they felt a sense of anticipation mixed with newfound peace. Leo knew that his journey didn't end with his own growth. He wanted to share this wisdom with the village, to help others find the balance he now cherished. Alongside Iris and Callum, he prepared to teach the villagers, knowing that some would be skeptical, just as he once had been.

When they entered the village, people gathered around them, eager to hear about their journey. Leo explained the concept of the Compass and Heart Map, sharing his insights and the challenges he had faced. He was honest about his struggles and open about the value of balance, showing them that balance wasn't just an idea—it was a way to enrich their lives.

One by one, villagers approached him, curious about how they could integrate balance into their own lives. He spoke with Marta, the baker who had always been practical, focused on routines and efficiency, often ignoring her own dreams. Leo encouraged her to let the Heart Map guide her occasionally, suggesting she try new recipes or take time to appreciate the beauty of her work.

He also spoke with Dax, a young artist who lived by his emotions, often leaving projects unfinished as his heart pulled him from one passion to the next. Leo guided him to use his Compass to set small goals, showing him that a little structure could help him fulfill his creative visions.

Over the following weeks, Leo saw a transformation in the village. People began to approach their lives with a new perspective, learning to blend practicality with passion. They helped each other, sharing experiences of balance and growth. Leo noticed how this harmony spread through the community, creating a place where people felt more fulfilled, where purpose and joy coexisted.

His teachings took root not just in individuals but in the village's collective spirit. Elders became mentors, guiding the youth on how to navigate life with both clarity and courage. Artists and tradesmen collaborated, combining their strengths in ways they hadn't considered before. Leo saw his vision becoming a reality—a village where balance was more than just an idea; it was a way of life.

In the evenings, as the village gathered around the fire, Leo would share stories from his journey, reminding them that balance wasn't something achieved overnight. It was a lifelong practice, a dance between logic and intuition, caution and courage. His words resonated, and he saw the quiet determination in their eyes, each of them inspired to walk their own path to balance.

As Leo looked out over the village, he felt a profound sense of peace. His journey to the Lost Glade had changed him, but more than that, it had given him a gift he could share. He no longer needed to prove anything or seek validation; he simply trusted himself and his path.

One night, as he stood by the edge of the village with Iris and Callum by his side, he shared his final thoughts with them.

"Balance isn't a destination. It's a journey that changes you along the way," he said, his voice calm and full of warmth. "Each step teaches you something new, and each person you meet offers a piece of the puzzle. Keep following your Compass, trust your Heart Map, and remember that you're never truly alone on this path."

With those words, Leo's journey to balance was complete, not because he had reached an endpoint, but because he had embraced the beauty of the journey itself.

Chapter 13: Mapping New Paths

Returning to the village after his transformative journey, Leo felt as if he were seeing his home with new eyes. The familiar landscapes, the winding paths through the woods, the streams and fields he'd grown up near—all these places seemed to hold hidden dimensions now. Each route, each bend in the road, each clearing in the forest appeared to offer more than he had once imagined. He realized that the maps he had created over the years—those neat, precise routes through familiar terrain—now seemed limited. They were incomplete, not because they were inaccurate, but because they captured only one aspect of the world.

With the Compass in one hand and his Heart Map in the other, Leo understood that the time had come to expand his maps, to reflect the fullness of his journey. The maps, after all, had always been more than just practical tools to him. They were symbols of discovery, markers of the paths that led to new experiences, insights, and connections. Now, he was ready to chart a new kind of map, one that would show others how to navigate with both the Compass and the Heart Map, balancing logic and intuition to explore life's vast array of possibilities.

Word had quickly spread through the village about Leo's adventures and the wisdom he had brought back. Villagers, young and old, were eager to hear about the mythical Lost Glade, the Crystal of Balance, and the treasures of knowledge he had gained along the way. It was a crisp autumn morning when Leo called for a gathering in the village square, inviting everyone to come and hear about his journey and to learn the lessons that had transformed him.

The square was bustling with excitement as people gathered. Children sat on the grass at the front, wide-eyed with curiosity, while the elders found seats nearby, leaning forward to catch every word. Friends and neighbors filled the space, murmuring to each other as they eagerly awaited Leo's story.

When the crowd had settled, Leo stood before them with his Compass and Heart Map held high. "Many of you know I've been away, searching for answers," he began, his voice clear and calm. "I went in search of guidance and clarity, and what I found was something far more valuable—balance. Today, I want to share with you the tools that helped me along the way and show you how they can open up new possibilities in your own lives."

Leo walked over to a large table he had set up with blank sheets of parchment, ink, and quills. "Today, we are going to start mapping new paths—paths that reflect not just the landmarks and safe routes we know, but also the possibilities we have yet to explore."

Leo began by spreading out his old maps on the table. These maps, carefully crafted over the years, detailed every known path in and around the village. Villagers looked on, some recognizing paths they had traveled many times, others marveling at the intricacy of the details Leo had captured. He traced one path with his finger, a route through the forest that led to a beautiful lake.

"This path," he said, gesturing to it, "I've walked many times. But on my journey to the Lost Glade, I learned that there is more than one way to reach a destination. Each path can lead us to different experiences, even if the destination is the same."

He then opened his Heart Map, the delicate, glowing parchment filled with patterns that seemed to pulse gently in the light. The villagers gazed at it in awe, for it was unlike any map they had ever seen. It was less structured, almost organic, like the branches of a tree, with routes that twisted, turned, and sometimes even spiraled back on themselves.

"Unlike the Compass, which shows a single, direct path, the Heart Map illuminates paths I hadn't considered. It reveals opportunities for adventure, new encounters, and deeper connections. I realized that my maps were incomplete because they showed only the practical paths, not the ones led by intuition or feeling. But together, these maps—these tools—open us to both clarity and possibility."

He then began drawing on a blank sheet, tracing a route that combined both maps. The villagers watched as he added new paths that looped away from the main routes, paths that didn't follow the shortest distance or the easiest terrain but promised new experiences. He encouraged everyone to come forward, inviting them to add their own routes, places of interest, or favorite trails.

As each villager took their turn, they began to see that there was no single correct way to map their lives. Marta, the village baker, added a path leading to a hidden patch of wildflowers she had found in the hills, a place she went to for peace and inspiration. "I never thought to put this on a map," she said, a little shyly, "but it's where I go to gather my thoughts. It may not be practical, but it's meaningful."

Leo nodded with a smile. "That's exactly it, Marta. The Compass shows us practicality, but the Heart Map reveals meaning. Together, they guide us to a fuller life."

Callum added a route to a hilltop where he often played his music, a place with a view of the stars that inspired his songs. Iris sketched a path that wound through the forest to a quiet glade where she could sit in silence and reflect. These places, each deeply personal, would never have been included on a standard map. But here, they found a place, marked not just as destinations but as paths of the heart.

As more villagers added their paths, Leo's map began to take on a life of its own, a beautiful tapestry of possibilities, each line representing a different journey, a different perspective. The villagers started to see their village differently. The roads they walked every day took on new meaning, the forest became filled with hidden paths, and the streams and hills they'd grown up near felt imbued with new stories and possibilities.

Among the crowd, Leo noticed a group of children watching with eager eyes. He smiled and invited them forward, handing them a small piece of parchment and a quill. "Why don't you map out the places that feel special to you?" he suggested.

One of the boys, Jory, took the quill and quickly sketched a winding path through the woods to a hollow tree where he and his friends hid their treasures. A little girl named Lila drew a line from her house to a sunny field where she loved to watch the butterflies. Each child, in their own way, contributed to the map, adding their own sense of wonder and exploration.

"This isn't just about getting from one place to another," Leo told the children, his voice warm and encouraging. "It's about discovering all the possibilities around you. You might walk the same path a hundred times, but with your Heart Map, you'll notice something new each time. Life is full of surprises if you're open to seeing them."

The children beamed, their enthusiasm infectious, and Leo felt a surge of hope. He knew that by teaching the next generation to embrace both their Compass and their Heart Map, he was sowing the seeds for a village of dreamers and explorers, each one equipped to navigate life with balance and curiosity.

As the days went on, Leo continued to work with the villagers, encouraging them to explore their world with an open mind and heart. He hosted evening gatherings where they shared stories of their adventures, both large and small. Villagers began to speak about new places they had visited, routes they had never considered before, and the personal discoveries they made along the way.

One evening, Marta shared how she had taken a winding path to gather herbs for her baking. "It was a longer route, but I found a grove of elder trees," she said, her voice full of excitement. "I never would have known it was there if I hadn't followed my Heart Map."

Dax, the artist, shared how he had found a secluded spot by the river that inspired his latest painting. "I was never much for planning, but the Compass gave me a sense of direction, and the Heart Map let me wander freely. It's strange, but I feel like I'm creating from a deeper place now."

Leo listened, a quiet joy filling him as he watched his friends and neighbors come alive with new insights and possibilities. The village had become a place of discovery, each person finding their own way to blend logic and intuition, stability and adventure. It was a transformation that extended beyond the physical paths they walked; it was a shift in their outlook on life itself.

As Leo continued helping others map their paths, he came to a realization: his journey wasn't over. The Heart Map and Compass had more to teach him, and there were paths he had yet to walk. The Lost Glade and the Crystal of Balance were not final destinations but stepping stones in a lifelong journey of growth and learning.

One evening, as he sat alone in his home, looking over his new, expanded map of the village, he felt a pull toward a distant part of the forest, a place he had yet to explore. His Heart Map glowed softly, guiding him once again toward the unknown. This time, he knew he would follow—not because he needed answers, but because he had learned to trust the journey itself.

In the following days, Leo spoke to his friends about his desire to continue exploring, to seek out new places and new experiences beyond the village. The villagers understood, for he had shown them the importance of being open to possibilities. With warm embraces and heartfelt wishes, they sent him off, knowing that he would return with more stories, more wisdom, and perhaps even new paths to add to their ever-growing map.

As he stepped onto the road, Leo looked back one last time, a sense of peace washing over him. He knew he had left a legacy in the village—a legacy of balance, of blending head and heart, of mapping not only the roads that lay before them but the limitless paths within.

Chapter 14: The New Pathfinders

In the weeks that followed Leo's return to the village, a profound change took hold among the people. It began slowly, a shift as quiet and steady as dawn breaking over the hills, but soon it became impossible to ignore. The villagers, inspired by Leo's journey and the knowledge he shared, had begun to chart their own courses. For the first time, they were navigating life's familiar paths—and new ones—with a balance between head and heart.

The Compass, once regarded as the ultimate guide to efficiency and logic, was now paired with the Heart Map, a tool many had initially seen as strange or even impractical. As more villagers embraced this dual way of navigating, they discovered new experiences and perspectives, each one deepening their understanding of the world around them. It was as if the village itself had come alive, each path filled with the whispers of exploration and new possibilities.

Leo watched these transformations unfold with quiet pride, recognizing that he had sparked a gentle revolution. But as the days went by, he began to understand that this was no longer just his journey; it was the beginning of something far greater. His village, once content with routine and predictability, had become a community of explorers, each person a pathfinder in their own right.

One of the first to take up the call of exploration was Dax, a reserved villager who had long prided himself on his commitment to routine. Known for his methodical approach to life, Dax had always risen before dawn to fetch water from the river. His route was the same every morning: a straight path from his cottage to the water's edge, efficient and reliable.

But inspired by Leo's story, Dax decided to try something different. One morning, just as the sun began to color the sky with hints of orange and pink, he picked up his Compass as usual but also unfurled his newly created Heart Map. The Heart Map, more delicate and intuitive than his Compass, suggested a winding path along the river's edge, a path Dax had never considered. Curious, he decided to follow it.

As he walked, he noticed things he had overlooked before: a small grove of trees with birds singing, their notes filling the cool morning air; a patch of wildflowers, vibrant against the dewy grass; the soft murmur of the river weaving through rocks and reeds. The sights and sounds filled him with a sense of peace he hadn't felt in years. For the first time, Dax realized that his morning routine could be more than a chore; it could be a moment of beauty, a quiet celebration of the day's beginning.

Over the following days, Dax continued to follow his Heart Map each morning, his route changing slightly with each walk. Sometimes, he would take a detour through a meadow or stop by a grove to watch the light filtering through the trees. He no longer rushed to fetch the water and return but allowed himself to wander, to explore. He felt as if he had rediscovered the world around him, a world he thought he had known. His mornings became not just a task to complete but a source of inspiration and joy.

Word of Dax's newfound routine spread quickly through the village, and before long, others joined him. Groups of villagers began rising early to explore their own Heart Maps, setting off along new paths each morning, discovering secret gardens, hidden glades, and quiet streams they had never seen before. The river, once a silent witness to their daily chores, became a gathering place for stories, laughter, and reflection.

The village market, typically bustling with the same familiar faces and vendors, also began to change. Marta, the baker, noticed a difference in her customers. Rather than buying the same loaf of bread or the same pastries they always did, people were asking questions about new ingredients, unfamiliar flavors, and different recipes. Inspired by her Heart Map, Marta herself had begun experimenting with wild herbs and spices she'd gathered from the forest, introducing breads infused with hints of rosemary and thyme, pastries filled with seasonal berries, and cakes decorated with edible flowers.

Her stall, once predictable and straightforward, had transformed into a display of creativity, and villagers flocked to see what new delights she had crafted. She noticed that her customers no longer came just to buy bread; they came to talk, to share ideas, and to suggest new flavors and combinations. Some even brought their own foraged herbs, excited to see what Marta would create with them.

The market square, once a place of hurried transactions, had become a vibrant exchange of ideas. The villagers began sharing stories of their adventures, of paths they had taken off the beaten track, and of discoveries that had brought them joy or surprise. Conversations flowed freely, and there was a palpable energy, a sense of connection that hadn't existed before. People lingered, savoring the market as a place not just for trade, but for community and inspiration.

Not all who embraced the Heart Map's guidance took to it easily. Some found themselves challenged by the unpredictability and vulnerability it required. Callum, the village woodworker, had always trusted his hands and his tools, relying on precision and accuracy to create finely crafted furniture. He had little patience for anything that disrupted his focus, and the idea of the Heart Map had initially seemed frivolous to him.

But one day, feeling the curiosity sparked by Leo's stories, Callum decided to take a different route home from his workshop. His Heart Map guided him along a winding path through the forest, far from the straightforward route he usually took. As he walked, he found himself surrounded by towering trees and thick underbrush, the air filled with the scent of pine and moss. He was nervous at first, unused to the unpredictable terrain, but something compelled him to keep going.

As he ventured deeper, he came upon a fallen tree, its roots twisted and exposed. Callum's eye was immediately drawn to the intricate patterns in the wood, the knots and whorls telling a story of resilience and growth. He knelt down, tracing the lines with his fingers, marveling at the natural beauty he would never have noticed on his usual route. In that moment, he realized that there was more to craftsmanship than precision; there was also beauty in imperfection, in the organic shapes and textures that nature offered.

Inspired, Callum began incorporating these natural elements into his work. His furniture, once known for its perfect lines and symmetry, began to take on a new character, blending structured design with raw, unpolished beauty. His pieces became sought after, each one unique and filled with a sense of warmth and authenticity. Callum, once resistant to change, had become a pathfinder in his own right, finding balance between control and spontaneity.

The children of the village, too, were captivated by the Heart Map's allure. Unencumbered by the routines and responsibilities of adulthood, they embraced its possibilities with boundless enthusiasm. In groups, they set off on adventures, discovering hidden nooks and secret clearings, creating stories and games inspired by the places they found.

They named each path and place, filling the village with new landmarks: "Whispering Tree," where they told secrets to the leaves; "Fox's Hollow," where they imagined the woodland creatures lived; and "Magic Pool," where the reflections on the water's surface seemed to change with every visit. The village, once mapped with only practical routes, had transformed into a playground of imagination and discovery.

The parents, watching their children explore, began to realize the value of curiosity and wonder. They joined their children on their Heart Map adventures, seeing the village through their eyes, and discovering that the world held much more magic than they had remembered. Families began spending more time together outdoors, the boundaries between work and play blurring as they embraced the journey over the destination.

As more villagers took up the Heart Map alongside their Compass, a subtle but profound shift settled over the community. Tasks that had once been approached with routine efficiency—gathering firewood, fetching water, tending to crops—now became opportunities for exploration and reflection. People discovered joy in the mundane, finding beauty and meaning in places they had once overlooked.

Paths they had once considered unimportant or even troublesome now offered experiences that brought them closer to each other and to themselves. They learned that some paths required patience and caution, while others demanded courage and curiosity. By embracing both their heads and their hearts, the villagers found themselves growing, becoming more adaptable, more open to change, and more connected to one another.

Leo, observing this quiet revolution, felt a deep sense of fulfillment. He had started his journey seeking answers for himself, but his discoveries had sparked a transformation in the entire village. People were not just exploring new paths; they were exploring new ways of thinking, of being. The Heart Map and Compass had become part of the village's identity, tools that encouraged balance and curiosity, reason and wonder.

The village, once a place of predictable routines, had become a community of pathfinders, each person guided by their own unique blend of logic and intuition. Leo knew that this was only the beginning—that as the villagers continued to explore and discover, they would find new depths within themselves and each other.

As time went on, the Heart Map and Compass became treasured symbols of the village's culture, passed down through generations. Parents taught their children not only to follow the Compass's clarity but also to listen to the Heart Map's quiet wisdom. Children grew up

THE HEART'S MAP AND THE MIND'S COMPASS 85

with a respect for balance, understanding that the greatest discoveries were often found off the beaten path.

The village itself began to reflect this newfound spirit of exploration. Trails branched off in every direction, some leading to quiet places of reflection, others to bustling centers of activity. The once small, self-contained community had transformed into a vibrant, ever-evolving place, its map filled with possibilities. Leo's legacy had become part of the village's very soul, a reminder that life's richest paths are often the ones we choose to create ourselves.

Leo, now older and wiser, continued to walk these paths, grateful for the journey he had begun and for the journeys that others were beginning each day. As he looked out over the village, he saw a community that was not just surviving but thriving—a community that understood the power of balance, of blending head and heart, of finding the courage to map new paths and the wisdom to follow them.

Chapter 15: The Legacy of Balance

Years had passed, and the village that Leo once knew had grown in ways he could hardly have imagined. Paths wound through forests and meadows, trails that didn't simply connect one place to another but also bridged the journeys of the villagers' lives—each path a story, each route a reminder of the lessons learned. Leo, now an elder whose hair had turned silver with age, had become a beloved figure in the village, a source of wisdom and guidance, especially for the younger generation.

Leo's journey had left a profound impact, and his presence, calm and encouraging, continued to inspire everyone who crossed his path. His maps, carefully drawn over the years, were treasured artifacts. These were not ordinary maps but intricate weavings of places known and unknown, routes that blended the logic of his Compass with the insight of his Heart Map. They served as a foundation for the village's expanding understanding of what it meant to journey through life. They were, to the villagers, a testament to the art of balance—a blend of heart and mind, wisdom and wonder.

Now, Leo found himself at the heart of a new purpose: passing on the legacy of balance he had so painstakingly cultivated. With each story he told, each map he gifted, and each lesson he shared, he hoped to inspire a new generation to embrace the journey with both head and heart.

Leo's cottage, tucked away at the edge of the forest, had become a place of pilgrimage for young villagers eager to learn. His walls were lined with maps—maps that showed not only the practical routes but also paths that required intuition and courage. Each map was marked with small symbols, reminders of the places where he had encountered lessons and insights.

THE HEART'S MAP AND THE MIND'S COMPASS

One day, as the golden afternoon light filtered through his window, a group of children gathered around Leo's old wooden table, eager for a story. Among them were Elara, a curious girl with a sharp mind, and Finn, a boy with a big heart and a talent for drawing. Leo watched them with a smile; he saw the same spark in their eyes that he had once felt himself.

"Leo, tell us about this one," Elara said, pointing to a map marked with a spiral trail that led deep into the forest. The spiral symbol was familiar to all villagers now; it was the symbol of a journey inward, a path that was as much about self-discovery as it was about reaching a destination.

"This path," Leo began, "is where I first learned that not all journeys lead outward. Some paths take you deeper within yourself. It was there that I found the Crystal of Balance and understood the importance of blending head and heart."

The children listened intently, captivated by the tale. Leo explained that the path had been challenging, filled with moments of doubt and uncertainty. But he had learned that sometimes the answers lay not in moving forward but in looking within, in trusting both logic and intuition.

As he spoke, Leo's words painted vivid images in the children's minds: of the towering trees that had once seemed impenetrable, the hidden glade that had revealed itself only when he allowed himself to follow his heart, and the Crystal of Balance that had illuminated the beauty of harmony between thought and feeling.

The children sat in silence, absorbing the story. For Leo, these tales were more than memories; they were pathways he could pass on, guiding the younger generation to seek balance in their own journeys.

Elara was one of Leo's most frequent visitors, a girl known for her quick thinking and curiosity. She often came with questions that challenged Leo, questions that kept his mind sharp and reminded him of the importance of nurturing young minds. One day, however, Elara arrived at Leo's cottage with a troubled expression.

"What's on your mind, Elara?" Leo asked gently.

Elara hesitated, glancing down at her feet. "I have to choose a path," she said. "My family wants me to join the village council. They say I'd be good at it because I'm logical and thoughtful. But...I've always dreamed of being an explorer, like you. I want to go beyond the village, to find new places and draw my own maps. I don't know which path to choose."

Leo studied her for a moment, his eyes thoughtful. He saw a reflection of his younger self in her, the same struggle between duty and desire, between logic and passion. He took out two objects: his old Compass, worn from years of use, and his Heart Map, a newer version he had crafted with the lessons of his journey.

"Both the council and the path of an explorer are valuable paths, Elara," Leo said. "But the answer lies not in choosing one over the other. Instead, consider how you can bring both together."

Elara looked puzzled. "How can I do both?"

Leo smiled. "The council may need someone who can guide them with both wisdom and creativity. What if you joined the council but continued to explore, charting new paths not just for yourself, but for the village as well? You can bring what you discover into your work and show others the importance of balance."

Elara's face brightened as understanding dawned on her. "So...I don't have to choose just one?"

"Life rarely demands that we choose only one path, Elara," Leo replied. "The art of balance means finding ways to bring our passions and responsibilities together. The journey of life is rich because it allows us to be many things at once."

With newfound clarity, Elara decided to embrace both paths. She would serve her village while continuing her exploration, confident that she could navigate each journey with both her head and her heart.

In the years that followed, Leo dedicated himself to teaching the art of mapmaking to the younger generation. But his lessons went beyond drawing lines and marking trails. He taught the children to listen, to pay attention not just to the landmarks around them but also to the feelings and intuitions that arose within them.

Finn, the boy with a talent for drawing, had a gift for capturing emotions in his maps. His maps were not just records of where he had traveled but reflections of how each journey had made him feel. He learned to mark places of joy, fear, courage, and wonder, creating maps that were as much emotional as they were geographical.

One day, while Finn was working on a map of the forest, Leo joined him, observing the boy's careful work.

"What are you marking here?" Leo asked, pointing to a symbol that looked like a small flame.

"That's the place where I felt brave," Finn replied, his eyes lighting up. "It's where I decided to cross the river, even though I was scared."

Leo nodded approvingly. "That's an important moment to remember. Your maps will guide others, not just in where to go but in how to journey."

As Finn continued his work, Leo felt a deep satisfaction. He saw that the next generation was not only embracing the art of balance but also adding their own insights, deepening the village's understanding of what it meant to be both explorer and guide.

Over time, the village itself became a tapestry of paths, each one a story, a memory, a lesson in balance. The villagers, young and old, began to see their lives not as a single journey but as a collection of smaller journeys, each one a thread in the larger fabric of the community.

Paths once walked in isolation were now woven together by shared experiences and shared wisdom. Trails wound through the village, connecting homes, markets, and gathering places, each path marked by a symbol or memory that reminded the villagers of the values they had learned from Leo's journey.

One path was known as "The Path of Courage," leading to a hill where villagers often went to gain perspective on their lives. Another path, "The Spiral of Reflection," wound around a small grove where people would pause to meditate and seek clarity. There was even a path called "The Heart's Crossing," which led to a secluded spot by the river where villagers shared their deepest dreams and fears.

The village had transformed, not through grand changes or monumental events, but through the quiet, steady practice of balance. The villagers had become pathfinders in their own right, using both the Compass and the Heart Map to guide them, to create a life that was rich, connected, and deeply meaningful.

As Leo grew older, he became known as the village's Elder Pathfinder. His wisdom was sought by everyone, from the youngest children to the oldest villagers. But Leo always emphasized that the true legacy he hoped to leave was not himself or his maps but the understanding that balance was something each person must cultivate for themselves.

One afternoon, as Leo sat by the river surrounded by villagers, he shared what he called his "final lesson."

"We each carry a Compass and a Heart Map within us," he said, his voice steady but filled with emotion. "These tools are not just for journeys across the land, but for journeys within ourselves. The Compass reminds us to think, to plan, to be practical. The Heart Map reminds us to feel, to dream, to trust our instincts. When we bring these together, we find paths we never knew existed."

He looked around at the faces of those he had taught, faces filled with gratitude and understanding.

"As you journey through life, remember this: the paths you choose shape not only your own life but the lives of those who come after. Walk with balance, so that others may follow with trust and wonder."

The Next Chapter: A Village United by Balance

When Leo passed away years later, the village gathered to honor his memory. They celebrated his life not with sorrow but with joy, for his legacy lived on in every path, every map, every journey they undertook. They shared stories of the ways Leo's teachings had shaped their lives, of the courage they had found, the dreams they had pursued, the balance they had embraced.

Leo's maps were preserved as treasures, kept in a place of honor where villagers could come to learn and be inspired. The young pathfinders he had mentored continued to guide the village, teaching the next generation to walk with balance, to seek both wisdom and wonder in all that they did.

And so, the village continued to thrive, united by the legacy of balance—a legacy that reminded them that life's richest journeys were those walked with both head and heart, with both courage and caution, with both vision and love. The paths Leo had once walked alone were now traveled by many, a testament to the power of one person's journey to create lasting, meaningful change.

A New Compass, A New Map

In the years since Leo's passing, the village had blossomed, its people deeply rooted in the wisdom of balance that Leo had so lovingly nurtured. The paths he had charted were now familiar trails, traveled not only for their destinations but also for the lessons they offered along the way. However, the most profound transformation was in the village's approach to life itself; every journey, big or small, was approached with an understanding of the balance between heart and mind. Leo's legacy continued to shape lives, and it was in the eager, shining eyes of the village's children that this legacy found its fullest expression.

As tradition now dictated, each child in the village received their own Compass and Heart Map upon reaching a certain age. The ritual had become a rite of passage, a symbolic moment that marked the beginning of their lifelong journey toward understanding and harmony. On a clear, crisp morning, the newest group of children gathered in the village square, their eyes wide with excitement, their spirits brimming with dreams of adventure and discovery.

Among them were Arin, a bright boy with a fierce curiosity, and Mira, a gentle girl with an intuitive sense of wonder. As they received their Compasses and Heart Maps from the village elders, they held these objects with reverence, understanding that they were more than simple tools. To them, the Compass was a symbol of wisdom and logic, a guiding star for practical decisions. The Heart Map, on the other hand, was a delicate invitation to listen to the quiet, inner voices that so often knew the way forward, even when it seemed unclear.

After the ceremony, the children were led to a small hall near the edge of the village where Leo's maps were displayed. The room was quiet, filled with a sense of history and wonder. Leo's maps, though worn from years of use and touch, retained their magic; each line, symbol, and note was imbued with the spirit of a man who had journeyed not only across the land but into the depths of his own heart and mind.

The children gathered around the maps, drawn to the intricate details. Arin pointed to a winding path that led to the Crystal of Balance, his eyes lighting up as he whispered, "This is where Leo found the Crystal that showed him how to balance his mind and heart."

Mira, standing beside him, traced her fingers along a trail that ended at the Heart's Crossing, a secluded spot by the river. "And here is where people go to listen to their dreams and hopes," she murmured, feeling a deep resonance with the idea.

An elder named Sage Rowan, who had been one of Leo's closest friends, stepped forward. He had a kind face lined with age, and his voice carried a warmth that immediately put the children at ease.

"Leo's maps are guides," he began, "but remember, they are not your journeys. Each of you will find your own paths, your own places of learning, and your own symbols of balance. The Compass and Heart Map will be your companions, helping you as you navigate your own life."

The children nodded, understanding that their journeys would not simply be a retreading of Leo's footsteps but rather new trails, new stories, and new discoveries that would build upon his legacy.

In the days that followed, Arin grew particularly attached to his Compass. He admired its weight and the way it pointed north with unwavering precision. For Arin, the Compass was a source of certainty, a tool that offered guidance whenever he felt unsure. However, it also made him hesitant to consult his Heart Map, which felt less predictable, more abstract.

One evening, while exploring a path near the village, Arin met Sage Rowan by the river. Rowan noticed Arin's reliance on his Compass and gently asked, "Have you tried using your Heart Map, Arin?"

Arin hesitated. "I like my Compass better. It tells me where to go," he admitted. "The Heart Map just…shows me feelings. It doesn't tell me what's right or wrong."

Rowan smiled and placed a reassuring hand on Arin's shoulder. "The Compass shows you the direction, yes, but the Heart Map reveals the journey's purpose. Both are essential, Arin. They work together to help you find not only where you're going but why you're going there."

Arin thought about this deeply. Over the next few days, he began experimenting with his Heart Map, letting it guide him to places he hadn't planned to visit. He found that while the Compass could take him far, the Heart Map helped him understand the meaning behind his travels, enriching each experience in ways he hadn't anticipated.

Mira, on the other hand, was naturally drawn to her Heart Map. She would spend hours studying its gentle lines and symbols, feeling a deep connection to the intuitive guidance it offered. For Mira, the Heart Map was like a song that resonated within her, leading her to places and people that filled her with joy and wonder. However, her reliance on the Heart Map sometimes made her journey uncertain, as she often wandered off course, following feelings rather than clear directions.

One sunny afternoon, while Mira was exploring a forest trail, she realized she had lost her way. She tried to retrace her steps, but without a clear sense of direction, she became confused. Panic began to rise in her chest, and she wished she had her Compass to guide her back.

At that moment, she remembered Leo's lesson of balance. Taking a deep breath, she steadied herself and pulled out her Compass. By aligning it with her Heart Map, she was able to find her way back to a familiar path, her Heart Map now enriched by the practical guidance of the Compass.

The experience taught Mira a valuable lesson: though her Heart Map was a beautiful guide, the Compass was an essential partner, grounding her dreams and intuitions in practicality. From that day on, Mira carried both tools with equal respect, understanding that they could work in harmony to lead her to places she could only reach by listening to both her head and her heart.

As time went on, the children grew more adept at using their Compasses and Heart Maps together. They encouraged one another, sharing stories of their adventures and the ways in which each tool had guided them. They became known as the "New Pathfinders," children who were both explorers and teachers, embodying the balance of heart and mind that Leo had championed.

Under the guidance of the village elders, the New Pathfinders began creating their own maps, marking the places they had discovered and the feelings each journey had inspired. These maps were added to

THE HEART'S MAP AND THE MIND'S COMPASS 95

Leo's collection, expanding it with new routes, new symbols, and new meanings. It was a living legacy, one that continued to grow with each generation.

The children took pride in their role as the keepers of balance, knowing that their maps would one day guide others, just as Leo's maps had guided them. They understood that their journeys would not only shape their own lives but also the lives of those who would come after. In this way, they honored Leo's legacy, ensuring that his teachings would endure.

Years later, the village remained a place where balance was woven into the fabric of daily life. The paths that had once been Leo's personal journey had become a part of the village's collective wisdom. Each child who received a Compass and Heart Map understood that they were not just setting out on a physical journey but also embarking on an inner quest to find harmony between their head and heart.

The stories of Leo's life became cherished tales, passed down through generations. The New Pathfinders grew into wise adults, guiding the younger generation with patience and compassion, helping them understand that life's journey was not a choice between logic and intuition but a dance between the two.

In this way, Leo's legacy endured, a timeless beacon of balance. The Compass and Heart Map had become symbols of unity, reminders that every path we walk is enriched when we allow both reason and emotion to guide us. And so, the journey of balance continued, a journey that would always be new, always evolving, as each generation set out to find their own paths, shaped by both the wisdom of the past and the promise of the future.

Don't miss out!

Visit the website below and you can sign up to receive emails whenever Aariv Wadhwa publishes a new book. There's no charge and no obligation.

https://books2read.com/r/B-A-URNSC-KVKGF

BOOKS2READ

Connecting independent readers to independent writers.

Milton Keynes UK
Ingram Content Group UK Ltd.
UKHW030853151124
451262UK00001B/198